ERASED

JENNIFER RUSH

ERA

S E D

Ⓛ Ⓑ

Little, Brown and Company

New York   Boston

Little, Brown and Company

Hachette Book Group
237 Park Avenue, New York, NY 10017
Visit our website at www.lb-teens.com

Little, Brown and Company is a division of
Hachette Book Group, Inc.
The Little, Brown name and logo are trademarks of
Hachette Book Group, Inc.

The publisher is not responsible for websites (or their content)
that are not owned by the publisher.

First Edition: January 2014

Library of Congress Cataloging-in-Publication Data

Rush, Jennifer (Jennifer Marie), 1983–
Erased / Jennifer Rush.—First edition.
    pages cm.—(Altered)
Summary: "Seventeen-year-old Anna searches for answers about her past while she evades the Branch with genetically altered boys Sam, Cas, and Nick"—Provided by publisher.
ISBN 978-0-316-19715-1 (hc)
[1. Runaways—Fiction. 2. Memory—Fiction. 3. Genetic engineering—Fiction. 4. Identity—Fiction. 5. Science fiction.]
    I. Title.
PZ7.R89535Er 2013
[Fic]—dc23
2012048398

10 9 8 7 6 5 4 3 2 1

RRD-C

Printed in the United States of America

To Justin, my favorite brother

1

LIKE CLOCKWORK, I WOKE AFTER MID-
night and immediately had the urge to see Sam.

There was a moment, before I was fully alert, when I wondered if
it was safe to sneak down to the lab.

And then I remembered: We weren't at the farmhouse anymore.
There was no lab.

In order to see Sam, all I had to do was roll over.

He lay on his stomach, hands tucked beneath the pillow. In the
murky darkness, I could just make out the black lines of his birch tree
tattoo spreading across his back, the branches twining down his arms.

With my eyes, I traced the dimples made by bones and muscle in
his shoulders. Imagined what pencil I would use to sketch him on
paper. In the months since Sam, Nick, and Cas had escaped the

Branch's lab, and I'd gone with them, I'd learned that nothing was permanent, not even my memories. Now I took every opportunity to savor what I had, just in case.

Waste nothing was my new mantra. And I wouldn't. Not when it came to the boys. They were my family, blood or not. Cas was like my brother. And in some ways, so was Nick, even if we didn't necessarily like each other.

And Sam . . . well, I loved him more than anything.

I reached out to touch him, to check that he was solid and warm and real, but thought better of it. We'd all been on edge lately, and I worried that if I startled him, he'd go for the gun tucked beneath the mattress. And then point it at me.

As quietly and lightly as I could, I slipped from the bed and made my way down the stairs of our rented cabin. I found Nick hunched over the coffee table, a fire burning in the hearth beside him, silhouetting him in orange-and-red light. A dozen paper cranes lay in a pile at his feet. There was another in his hands.

He'd started folding them out of nowhere a little over a week ago and had given no reasonable explanation for it. The cranes he'd already made sat in a box beneath my bed because I didn't have the heart to throw them away.

"Hey," I said as I sat down across from him in one of the ratty leather chairs. "What are you doing up?"

He didn't look at me as he answered, "Why does anyone get up in the middle of the night? Because they can't sleep."

"Right."

His eyes were dark and swollen with exhaustion. His black hair stood in raked waves and curled around his ears. A green flannel shirt hugged his biceps and hung open, exposing the hard plane of his stomach.

Like all the boys, Nick, even at his worst, was gorgeous. It drove me crazy. I didn't consider myself unattractive, but next to them, I was painfully average. They didn't know the meaning of a bad hair day.

I grabbed the origami crane closest to me. The folds were precise. The tail point was razor-sharp. Everything about it was perfect. Nick, like Cas and Sam, rarely failed at anything.

"Any idea why you're doing this?" I tried.

Nick formed the head on the crane in his hands. "I don't know. I..." He trailed off, like he'd caught himself about to say something more revealing than he liked. He turned to me. "Why don't you run back to bed with your boyfriend and leave me alone?"

I frowned. The old me would have scurried away, but in the last few months, we'd made some progress on our relationship, if you could call it that. It helped that I knew Nick better now, knew the reason behind his cutting attitude. He'd grown up with an abusive father. But he didn't know that, not yet. The Branch had stolen those memories from him.

I'd wanted to tell him for a while now. I just didn't have the words to explain it.

3

"Sam isn't my boyfriend," I said, because it was the only thing I could think to say. "I mean, not officially." I grabbed one of the pre-cut squares of paper and started to fold. "Besides, I'm not tired."

Nick grumbled. "Whatever."

Outside, the wind whistled through the trees and rattled the front door. Snow had fallen not long after dinner. It was now piling in the corners of the windowsills.

Nick finished his crane and tossed it aside. He looked over at me. Normally, his eyes were shockingly blue, electric, but in the firelight, they were leaden gray and guarded. "What's with that look on your face?"

"What look?"

"Like you have something to say."

In some weird way, not having a closer relationship with Nick made him that much better at reading me. His judgment, his gut instinct, wasn't clouded by petty emotions. It made it ridiculously hard to hide anything from him.

I swallowed. "I don't know what you're talking about."

He sighed, exasperated. "Don't play dumb."

I made another fold in the paper, thinking while I worked. Finally, I said, "There are some things about your past...that maybe you should know."

"What, and you do?"

"I don't know much."

"But you know enough."

I stopped folding. "It might help you understand—"

"I understand plenty." He cracked a knuckle, then another. He avoided looking me in the face, and realization crept in.

"You're having flashbacks? About your—" I stopped myself, just in case. "The flashbacks are more substantial, aren't they? More detailed?"

Sam was the first one to experience memory flashes. Cas and Nick had been having only minor ones since we'd left the farmhouse nearly three months ago. And me, well, I was having them, too— mostly about my older sister, Dani.

When I'd first left home with the boys, I'd thought I was a normal girl swept up in their extraordinary lives, only to find out much later that I'd been altered, too, like them. That the Branch had buried all the important memories from my past life, thereby wiping my sister from existence.

We'd found out she'd been killed by the Branch, and since then, I'd tried so hard to remember her. She came to me in fleeting images and ghost feelings that I later tried to sketch and make real. I hadn't been successful yet. And lately, the flashbacks had been giving me the worst kind of headaches. Enough to send me straight to bed. I hadn't told Sam that part yet. I didn't want him to worry or treat me differently.

"So what are they about?" I asked Nick. "Tell me."

He clenched his hand into a fist, knuckles rising and turning white. "I'm not telling you anything. So stop asking." He said it matter-of-factly, like no earthly force would pry the details from his head. With Nick, it was probably true. In some ways, he was more stubborn than Sam.

He swept out of the chair, breezed past me without another word, and disappeared upstairs, his bedroom door shutting a second later.

The fire in the hearth snapped.

I set aside my half-folded crane and took the last one Nick had made, suspended it between my fingers. That's how Sam found me a minute later, motionless, staring at that stupid crane.

He ran his hand up and down his arm as if to ward off the cold. "What happened?" he asked.

I let the crane fall to the table. "I pissed him off."

Sam sighed as he sat. He looked so tired, even though he'd been sleeping more than all of us lately. It was so unlike him. "What was it about this time?"

I hadn't told anyone else the details I knew about Nick's past. It should be up to him who he shared it with. So I just shrugged and said, "Who knows." A yawn made me pause, then, "I think I'm going to lie back down."

Sam nodded, and I knew that meant he wasn't coming.

"If I'm not up by dawn, will you wake me?"

"Sure."

I started for the stairs, but as I passed him, he reached out, snagging me at the wrist. He pulled me down onto his lap, wrapped a hand around the back of my neck, and put his lips to my forehead. I closed my eyes, breathed him in. He smelled like Ivory soap and fresh air. He smelled like home.

I love you, Anna. He didn't have to say it for me to know that he meant it.

I met his gaze. *I love you, too,* I thought as I pulled away and headed upstairs.

2

WHEN I WOKE A FEW HOURS LATER, I could hear Cas singing a Celine Dion song in the shower down the hall. "My Heart Will Go On," from the sound of it.

I threw on a baggy sweater over a tank top and black leggings and headed downstairs. Sam sat at the small table tucked in the back corner of the kitchen, and Nick stood at the stove, scrambling up some eggs.

"Is there enough for me?" I asked.

"Yes," Sam answered before Nick could comment.

After fixing myself a cup of coffee, I sat beside Sam. He was on the laptop, presumably reading over the files we had procured from the Branch. Many of them spanned our entire involvement, from the time we entered the program to right before we left the farmhouse lab. It was going to take us more than a few months to read everything inside, but we were making good progress. Not that we'd found anything substantial yet. Sam's files were bigger than anyone else's. He'd been with the Branch the longest, sold into it by his mother. They started experimenting on genetic alterations with him and expanded from there.

"Anything new?" I asked, squashing the urge to read over his shoulder.

"Not really."

Nick sat across from me a minute later, his plate overflowing with eggs, two pieces of toasted bread beside the pile. He dug in without a word.

"I'll grab our plates," I said to Sam while shooting Nick a scowl. When I got to the stove, I found the pan nearly empty, so I divided what was left into three equal parts, leaving enough for Cas when he came down.

"We're out of eggs," Nick said. "Who's on grocery duty this week?"

"Me," I answered. "And you."

"Great."

I would have gone alone if Sam would have allowed it, but we'd agreed a long time ago that it was best if we traveled in pairs. Grocery shopping was always done with someone else, and we tried to stick to a constant rotation.

Sam downed the rest of his black coffee. "I'll go."

"No." I shook my head. "It's my turn. You and Cas went last

week." I took a bite of eggs, silently hoping he'd insist he go in my place.

But he didn't. I'd asked him to treat me like an equal. Apparently, I was now getting my wish.

"We'll go this afternoon," I said to Nick. "So don't disappear on me."

He tossed his empty plate in the sink and left.

My day was looking up already.

———————

It'd been over two months since we'd escaped the Branch and encountered any of its agents, but that didn't mean we could lower our guard. Everything we did was calculated and thoroughly planned out. Like who went grocery shopping and when. Who checked the perimeter and when.

But it couldn't be *too* planned out, because then the Branch would be able to predict our movements.

Sometimes just taking a shower seemed like far too much work. At Sam's insistence, I always locked the bathroom door behind me, made sure the window was unlocked for a quick alternate exit should I need it. And my gun stayed loaded on the vanity.

Living a normal life didn't seem possible, not with the Branch still out there. It was why we were always on edge. We couldn't relax. Ever. And the longer we went without seeing a Branch agent, the more we felt like our time was running out.

After breakfast, Sam and I got dressed for a perimeter check. He wore a thick black coat with a flannel shirt underneath, jeans, and black leather boots. I had bought a heavier coat a few weeks ago when winter settled in. It was graded for below zero temps. With it, I wore cold-weather leggings tucked into boots.

In the woods, we made our way from one checkpoint to another. I ducked beneath a pine branch and squinted as the sun appeared, the blinding rays reflecting off the snow-covered ground. I had sunglasses on, but they didn't help much.

If an agent attacked me right now, I'd be caught off guard, unable to see. I often found myself thinking about little things like that. And about how many weapons I had on me. Whether or not they were loaded or easy to grab. Right now I had a gun on my back and a knife sheathed in my boot. I could remember a time when one gun seemed like one weapon too many. Now I wished I had more.

Sam trailed behind me by a foot, his steps quiet despite the ice that'd formed on the snow overnight. Every step I took made a loud and annoying crunch.

"I've been meaning to talk to you," Sam said as we rounded a mammoth oak tree. "I think it's time we move again."

I glanced over my shoulder, pausing for a second as he caught up. "Already?"

He stopped beside me. "It's been four weeks."

We'd moved twice since we'd escaped the Branch. I understood why, but I was tired of settling into new places.

I wanted to have the opportunity to rebuild the life that had been stolen from me, and I knew that started with piecing together my past and learning more about my family. I couldn't do that if we kept moving, especially when it seemed like we were heading farther and farther away from Port Cadia, the town where I'd grown up. It was the place where my life and Sam's had been altered completely when he and I lost my sister.

I wanted to know how Dani died and what had happened to her body. I wanted to know why the Branch had killed my parents. I knew the Branch had put me in the farmhouse lab, in the Altered program, because I'd already had a connection to the boys, especially Sam. They'd used that connection and twisted it into something scientific, something they could reproduce and later sell.

But I still wasn't sure if they'd killed my parents so that I wouldn't have a family searching for me, or if there was another reason. We already knew they had the ability to wipe people's memories. So why not spare my parents and alter their memories instead?

We didn't know the endings to any of the important mysteries, and I desperately wanted to.

I *needed* to.

"Anna?" Sam called out.

I stopped walking. I hadn't even realized I'd moved. "Yeah?"

"You're two steps away from hitting that bear trap." He gestured at a lump in the ground.

"Oh. Thanks."

"You okay?" he asked.

"Fine." I bent over to inspect the trap, looking for any clues that it'd been tampered with or set off. The cold bit through my leather gloves, numbing my fingers as I worked. "So, where are we going this time?" I asked.

"I was thinking Indiana."

"Maybe we should move north."

Even when I wasn't looking directly at Sam, I could still feel the full weight of his gaze. It lifted the hair at the base of my neck.

"No" was all he said.

I sighed and kept walking. I wasn't sure how I'd convince him that learning more about our past was a good idea, because when Sam set his mind on something, he generally didn't budge. His number one priority was to keep us away from the Branch and keep us safe. Obviously I valued my life, but it didn't feel like much of a life with so many of the pieces still missing.

And hadn't Sam been the one to finally break free of the lab, only to risk his safety and freedom again when it was his past he was trying to figure out?

Of course, there was one common denominator in all of this. The whole reason Sam had gone to so much trouble *before* the farmhouse, the whole reason he'd had clues to retrace in the first place.

Dani.

The sister who had been stolen from me.

Sam's old girlfriend.

Dani was a huge part of Sam's past. I knew he was curious to fill in the blanks surrounding her death, even if he wouldn't admit to it. And finding out more information about her would also give me more information about my family and *my* past.

It didn't escape me, though, that I was in love with my sister's old boyfriend, and that if she were alive, Sam and I probably wouldn't be together.

What if digging into our pasts reminded Sam of what he'd lost with Dani? What if it brought on the guilt that was already creeping into my thoughts?

And what would that mean for us?

I wasn't sure if I was willing to take that risk.

3

NICK BACKED INTO A PARKING SPOT in the grocery store lot, facing the SUV toward the exit so we could escape quickly if we needed to. Out of habit, I scanned the lot and the street beyond, pausing on anyone who looked suspicious.

There was a woman hurrying a child down the sidewalk, both of them hunched against the wind.

A gray-haired man got out of his sedan in front of the paper goods store and raced inside. A small black truck with tinted windows crawled past the grocery store. It might have been suspicious, but the streets were slick with snow and salt, making traveling over thirty miles an hour almost impossible. Regardless, Nick and I watched as it rounded the next corner.

"Are we good?" I asked.

Nick checked his rearview mirror one more time before pulling the keys out of the ignition. "We're good."

I hurried toward the store, arms clasped tightly in front of me, trying to ward off the wind. Inside, I grabbed a cart as Nick sauntered up behind me.

Without saying a word, we started down the first aisle, where all the discounted items were, and started picking things off our list. While Sam still had cash on reserve, we were trying to be smart with the money we had left, and food generally came in second behind weapons. Food could be stolen if it came down to it, but guns were harder to come by. You couldn't pluck a gun off a gas station shelf while someone distracted the store clerk.

At the end of the sale aisle, I paused to look at a display of winter gear. I'd been running every day but was finding it more difficult in the colder air. My throat tightened up too quickly, and my lungs burned. I couldn't make it a full 5k without having to walk.

I grabbed something called a neck gaiter and held it out in front of me. It was really nothing more than a tube of fleece meant to cover half your face. That'd help keep my throat and lungs warm.

Nick nodded at the gear when I tossed it in the cart. "What are you getting that for?"

"To help me run better."

He snatched it from the cart and hung it back up. "Don't train yourself into a crutch. You think the Branch is going to wait for you to"—he read the tag—"put your neck gaiter on before chasing you down?"

I gave the fleece a wistful look. Nick was right, of course, and that only annoyed me more.

Halfway through the store, Nick disappeared, but I didn't bother looking for him. I was happier shopping alone anyway. I filled the cart with the necessities, making good time. Sam liked us to be in and out of the store in less than thirty minutes. As I headed into the condiments aisle, I checked my list, tossing ketchup and mustard into the cart before crossing them off. I started for the peanut butter and grumbled when I found my favorite brand gone.

"Is there something I can help you find?"

I whirled around. A boy wearing one of the store's green uniforms stood behind me. His name tag read BRAD in crinkled sticker letters.

"Umm..." I pointed at the shelf over my shoulder. "Do you guys hold stock in the back? I'm looking for Mountain Valley peanut butter, and the shelf's empty."

The boy smiled, showing a crooked front tooth. "I can check. Hold on just a sec." He pulled a walkie-talkie from his belt, pressed a button, and said, "Lori, can you look up a UPC for me?"

The handheld crackled with static, and then a woman said, "Read me the numbers."

"You don't have to go to this much trouble," I said, and started backing up.

We were running out of time, and I still had to find Nick and check out. Who knew what Sam would do if we were gone longer than an hour.

"It'll just take a second," Brad said, and started rattling off a series of numbers into the walkie.

I checked both ends of the aisle. Sam had been teaching me surveillance techniques, and one of his biggest points was *Know your surroundings*.

The woman's voice sounded a second later. "Out of that product until the truck comes in."

"All right. Thanks." Brad turned to me. "I suppose you heard that."

I smiled. "I did. I appreciate you checking."

I pushed the cart forward, but Brad followed. "Are you new around here? I don't think I've seen you before. Do you go to Bramwell High?"

"No. I mean, yes, I'm new here, but I'm homeschooled. Or was. I'm done." That was a lie. I still had a few months left.

"Cool," Brad said as he clipped his walkie-talkie onto his belt. He shoved his hands in his pants pockets, causing him to hunch forward. He was quite a few inches taller than me, maybe six feet even. The same height as Sam.

"Do you live close to town?"

That question caught me off guard, and immediately all my senses went on alert. Was he asking because he was being friendly or because he was part of the Branch?

Fortunately, Nick appeared and answered for me. "She doesn't live anywhere close by. Come on, Frannie. We have to go."

Frannie? I frowned. *That was the best alias he could come up with?*

"Right. I'm coming, *Gabriel*," I said.

Nick narrowed his eyes. Gabriel was an alias he'd used before the farmhouse lab. We'd found mention of it in one of his old files. He detested that name. *"Sounds like the kind of guy I'd hate,"* he'd said.

Brad looked between Nick and me.

Cas once described Nick as a shark masquerading as a panther, which pretty much summed it up. Even strangers could pick up on Nick's terrible personality, or lack thereof, if he wasn't trying to hide it.

And right now, he wasn't.

Brad straightened his shoulders. Whether consciously or unconsciously, he was going into defense mode.

I could tell that Brad thought Nick was my boyfriend, which made me want to deny it quickly and vehemently. But then Nick put his arm around me and pulled me closer. The denial got stuck in my throat.

"Umm...thanks for your help," I said as Nick steered us away.

"No problem," Brad said quietly, still rooted in place.

When we were out of the aisle and on to the next, I shrank away from Nick. "Was that really necessary?"

He plucked a box of cereal off the shelf and tossed it in the cart. "Was *what* necessary?"

I sighed. "Sometimes I hate you."

"Yeah, well, the feeling is mutual." He grabbed a canister of rolled oats. "What were you doing, anyway? Chatting up the stock boy? You know better, *Frannie.*"

"I'm not a child, *Gabriel.*" I blew out an exasperated breath. "All I wanted was some peanut butter." I crossed cereal and oats off the list. "And I was handling it just fine before you showed up. I'm smarter than you seem to think."

"Maybe so, but you're not as prepared for any of this as the rest of us."

True. But I was learning. And I was willing to do whatever it took to *be* prepared.

We finished filling the cart and chose the only checkout lane that was open. It was run by a girl a few years older than me, with black hair and one stripe of cherry red in her bangs. A hoop pierced her lower lip and another hung from her left eyebrow.

When she saw Nick, she smiled, showing off a steel ball in the center of her tongue. "How are you today?" she asked him, totally ignoring me.

Nick might be surly around me, but he knew when and how to turn on the charm, and apparently now was one of those times.

He leaned a hip into the counter and crossed his arms over his chest, making his biceps bigger. He grinned. "I'm good. You?"

The girl shrugged. "It's been slow today. This place is so boring."

Nick laughed, the sound hoarse and deep. "This *town* is boring."

"Totally." The girl rolled her eyes, commiserating with him. "My friends and I go to the city almost every weekend just to escape."

Nick leaned in closer. "Where do you go?"

"Usually a club called DuVo. It's pretty rad."

Rad? Who uses that word?

I watched the register screen for the total and handed over enough cash to cover it.

"Maybe I'll check it out," Nick said.

"You totally should." The girl gave me the change and the receipt. "We'll be there tomorrow night for sure."

"What's your name?" Nick asked, using the excuse to check out the girl's chest, like he meant to find a name tag.

"Teresa," she said.

Nick smiled. "I'll see you later, Teresa."

She smiled back as I scooped up the shopping bags, twice as annoyed as I had been five minutes ago. If that was even possible.

In the parking lot, I threw the bags in the back of the SUV and slid into the passenger seat. "How do you do that, anyway?"

Nick stuck the key in the ignition, and the engine cranked to life. "Do what?"

"Act normal and fake."

"It's a learned skill."

"Are you really going to that club?" The question came out holding more weight than I meant it to. As much as Nick and I disliked each other, I still cared where he went and how long he was gone. Our relationship might have been dysfunctional, but it was safer to stick together. No one else could possibly understand what we'd gone through or what we still had to deal with every day.

I set an elbow on the door's arm rest and looked out the window, trying not to care what Nick's answer was.

"Maybe," he said as he pulled out of the parking lot. "Not that it's any of your business."

"Yes, it is. Because we have rules, and the rules are we don't separate."

He frowned at me briefly before turning his attention back to the road. "That's bullshit and you know it. I can manage just fine on my own."

"At the risk of dying."

He grunted. "Dying would be preferable to this conversation."

I sighed. Of course, we all had the right to leave the group whenever we wanted.

I hadn't thought any of us would actually do it, though.

4

I PULLED A QUILT OVER MY LAP AND propped myself up against the headboard of my bed, setting my journal on my knees. I flipped through the pages, my fingers coming away covered in graphite dust.

I stopped at a sketch of a boy with amber eyes, and my stomach clenched.

Trev.

He'd been the fourth boy in the farmhouse lab, and had been working undercover for the Branch all along. I had thought he was my best friend, but he'd turned on me when I'd needed him the most and put a gun to my head.

I closed my eyes as the memory came back. Some nights I dreamed that he'd pulled the trigger.

I missed him. Or at least the old him. More than I could admit to Sam or the others without feeling like a traitor.

Trev had been the one I went to when I needed advice. Especially when it came to Sam. Trev never made me feel weak, or silly, or any of the other things you'd think you'd feel growing up around four genetically altered boys.

To Trev, I'd been an equal, always.

I tried reminding myself that the Branch had wiped his memories, planting false ones in the void, just like they had with me. He'd believed he was working for the Branch to protect someone he loved.

If anyone understood what that felt like, it was me. But forgetting that he'd manipulated all of us and almost cost us our lives was another story.

With a pencil in my hand, I turned to a blank page and started roughing in a sketch, trying to banish all thoughts of Trev from my mind.

The idea for the sketch had come out of nowhere a few days before. I didn't know what it meant, but I couldn't shake the image, and I thought getting it out on paper might help to decode it.

I started with the foreground, because that was the clearest in my mind. There were two people on a porch overlooking a yard. It was just after dusk. They sat on the steps, hunched close, as if they were sharing secrets.

In the background was a line of tall, skinny trees, not unlike the birch trees that made up Sam's tattoo.

I'd seen the place that matched Sam's tattoo; it'd been not far from my childhood home, and this—the porch, the birch trees, it all seemed awfully familiar.

Was the sketch an old memory?

When I finished, I held up the journal.

The two people, though they were faced away, were a boy and girl. The boy was taller, older. His hair was a silhouette of loose curls against the landscape beyond the porch. The girl's hair was pulled back in a bouncy ponytail.

The girl was me.

I was almost sure of it. A phantom scent came to me, and I closed my eyes. The smell of wet earth. Of summer air. Of a boy.

Immediately I knew he was someone important to me. Or had been at one time. He was a feeling more than he was a specific person or face.

Sadly, I didn't know enough details about my biological family to know if he was a part of it. As far as I knew, I had only one sibling: Dani. But I supposed it could have been a neighbor or a cousin. These were the answers I wanted, the reasons I needed to look into my past.

Maybe someone else knew how Dani had died. Or maybe they knew more about our family.

After shutting the journal, I eased beneath the quilt and closed my eyes again, hoping something might come to me.

I pictured my old house, the bedrooms, the kitchen, the back porch.

In my head, I re-created the scene, trying to fill in the details that I hadn't been able to with my pencil, when a footstep sounded from the doorway.

I opened my eyes.

Sam stood inside the bedroom, a cup in each hand. "Hey," I said. "Aren't you supposed to be on watch?" It was late, and I'd heard Nick and Cas go to bed not too long ago. Whatever had brought Sam here was more important than him guarding the house, apparently. A thrill went up my spine until I saw the disquieted look on his face. All thoughts of the old memory faded.

Nudging the door shut, Sam came farther into the room. "I brought you something to drink."

I took the offered coffee. He didn't have to say anything for me to know he was worried about me. Probably because of my mistake earlier, during our perimeter sweep. This time I'd almost walked into a bear trap—next time it might be a Branch agent.

"I'm fine," I said. "I know you came up here to check on me."

He let out a breath and sat on the edge of the bed. "None of us are fine, Anna." He leaned over and set his coffee on the bedside table. "I know what I went through when I started having flashbacks. I know what it felt like to withdraw from the treatments they were giving us in the farmhouse. And who knows how it'll affect you. Your treatments were different from ours, and they weren't documented very well. We have nothing to go on." He paused, then said, "I just want to be sure you're feeling okay. Because if you're not—"

"I would be a liability."

He didn't say anything.

"I'm fine," I repeated. "I swear it."

He glanced at me over his shoulder. "I think you're lying."

"I think you're overreacting." I took a drink of coffee before putting the mug next to his on the table.

And that's when he lunged.

He grabbed me by the wrist and twisted, his back to my chest, flipping me over. A second later, he was on top of me, my arms pinned, his legs tight against my hips.

The springs in the bed squeaked and settled before I could catch my breath and comprehend what he was doing.

He was testing me.

And I'd failed.

I hadn't defended myself. I hadn't fought back. I hadn't *reacted* at all.

He leaned forward, eyes tight. "You. Are. Not. Fine."

"Of course I'm not going to fight you. I know you won't hurt me."

"Your brain shouldn't have had time to distinguish between enemy or friend. We've been training you. You had years of combat classes. Defending yourself, even against someone you care about, shouldn't be a secondary reaction. It should be your first."

I licked my dry lips. Sam's attention shifted downward, and heat touched my cheeks. I unclenched my hands, moving beneath him.

His hold lessened, and I felt his legs loosen. I seized the opening, arching my back. He lost his balance and pitched to the side, so I followed the movement, rolling us over so I pinned him.

Finally, he relaxed and grinned. It was a treat I didn't get often, and I found it ridiculously hot.

"Better?" I asked with an arch of my eyebrows.

"Better. But we still need to talk about what's going—"

I cut him off with the press of my lips. He tensed at first, but didn't stop me, and finally his hands moved downward to the curve of my butt, pulling me closer. I dropped forward as Sam's mouth sank lower, down my jaw, down my neck to my collarbone.

A board creaked on the first floor.

Sam and I both froze. My heart beat at every pulse point from the leftover thrill of Sam's body pressed against mine and the sudden adrenaline bursting through my veins.

Sam retrieved one of his guns from beneath the mattress and quietly pulled the slide, loading a bullet in the chamber. I rolled over, edged off the bed, and dropped to my knees, retrieving the gun I'd hidden beneath the bed frame.

Sam crept toward the door, hands wrapped around his gun. He put his back against the wall, taking the lead position. I grabbed the doorknob and pulled. The door opened silently. Sam had oiled every hinge and lock on the upstairs floor for this very reason, so we could move through the house undetected.

I counted to three in my head, and I knew Sam was doing the same. On three, he swung around the edge of the doorway, gun first.

The muscle in his forearms tensed. I followed him out, skipping over the floorboard stained from old water damage. That was the one that popped when walked across, and I'd made a mental note to avoid it ever since our first night here.

In the stairwell, we paused as a shadow crossed the moonlight spilling through a living room window. The front door creaked, followed by the soft click of the latch.

Sam took two steps down.

I echoed his movements, sticking close to the wall.

When the stairwell opened up, Sam crouched and waved for me to hold as he scanned the living room through the banisters.

He flicked two fingers a second later. All clear.

The descent down the remaining steps seemed to take forever, but when we finally hit the ground level, we broke up, Sam taking the left, toward the dining room, me the right, to the living room.

Since I already knew it was empty, I went straight for the windows and pushed aside the thick blackout curtains.

There were no vehicles out front other than ours. No Branch agents.

Just a lone person walking down the driveway.

I whistled, signaling Sam. He hurried to my side.

"Look," I whispered.

Sam glanced out the window. "It's Nick," he said. "What the hell is he doing?"

He tucked his gun in the waistband of his pants, threw open the front door, and jogged down the porch steps. I was only in a tank top and shorts. I pulled on a jacket and boots and thumped after him.

Thick snowflakes fell from the darkened sky. The night was eerily still, the snow covering everything in a blanket of pure silence so that every step I took seemed to echo through the woods.

"Where are you going?" Sam called to Nick.

"Out," Nick said, and kept walking.

"Nick. Wait." I caught up to him and Sam. "Can you come back inside and talk, please?"

"Talk?" He looked over at me, his eyebrows furrowed in irritation. "That's the problem, Anna. All you want to do is talk."

"Maybe because you never do." My teeth chattered against the cold, but it didn't stop the heat in my voice. "I've been living with you for two months, and I still know nothing about you other than you're a jerk and—"

He stalked over to me, putting his face just inches from mine. "Fine. Let's talk. Where do you want to start? How about we start with the fact that I can no longer tell what's real or not real? That I'm having flashbacks so often, I feel like I'm losing my goddamn mind?" He stopped only long enough for a breath. "Or maybe we can talk about how often my flashbacks end with dead people? People I killed? You have no idea what the Branch had us doing. And you don't *want* to know."

Sam edged between us. "Come on," he said quietly. "She's just trying to help."

Nick didn't take his eyes off me as he spoke. "I don't need her help. I don't need any of you."

He twisted back around and walked off. "What I need is some fucking space."

"How much?" Sam asked carefully. "A mile? A county? A state?"

Nick shoved his hands in his pants pockets. "As much space as I can get."

I glanced over at Sam.

"Are we just going to let him go?" I asked quietly.

Sam nodded. "If he needs space, let him have it. Nothing we say or do will change his mind."

Sam retreated inside. I stayed where I was, legs freezing, fingers numb, waiting for the moment when I could no longer see Nick.

He disappeared around a bend in the driveway, the darkness and the falling snow swallowing him up completely.

When I got inside, Sam resumed his position downstairs, keeping watch over the house, while I went upstairs to bed. With the quilt tucked around my shoulders and the house quiet, I hoped I'd fall asleep quickly enough so I didn't have to think about Nick.

But as soon as I closed my eyes and felt myself relaxing into the pillow, voices filled my head. A flash of white light shone behind my lids.

I knew immediately what it was: a flashback.

There was yelling.

A pink blanket beneath me.

A jewelry box open on the dresser.

A boy next to me on the bed.

"You okay?" he asked.

My hair fell forward, and I wiped at my eyes. I was crying. And I didn't want him to see me like this, like a baby.

He leaned in closer. "Anna?"

"Why are they yelling at each other?" I asked.

"Sam's mad about something your sister did, and your sister is a—" *He cut himself off, and I felt him watching me. He took a deep breath. "Never mind." He cleared his throat. "Do you want to see something my mom taught me?"*

I sniffed, wiped my face clean. "What is it?"

"You got any paper? I'll show you."

The voices faded. I dug for a piece of paper in my desk. A pretty red sheet with hearts on it. I handed it over, and the boy snorted.

"What?" I said.

He ruffled my hair. "Nothing. It's just, you're such a girl."

"Anna?" Fingers dug into my shoulders and shook. "Hey, wake up."

I opened my eyes. Sam was hunched over me, moonlight painting a lace pattern on his face. I couldn't tell how much time had passed since I'd gone to bed, but it seemed like hours.

"What?" I croaked.

"You were crying."

I swiped at my face. My hand came away wet.

"It must have been a bad dream," I answered. I looked over his shoulder, to the hallway. Cas's bedroom door stood open. "Cas on watch now?"

"Yeah."

"Will you lie down with me, then?"

He nodded and went around to the other side of the bed. I heard him set his gun on the table, felt the mattress shift as he double-checked the extra gun beneath it. He did that every night. Somehow it made me feel safer.

Out of the corner of my eye, I caught sight of his shirt being tossed aside, then felt him slide in next to me beneath the quilt. He wrapped an arm around my waist and drew me closer, planting a breath of a kiss on my bare shoulder.

" 'Night," I whispered.

"Good night."

When I fell asleep again, it was thankfully, blissfully, flashback-free.

5

TWO DAYS. IT'D BEEN TWO DAYS SINCE
Nick left. He hadn't even bothered to call. And the longer he was
gone, the more anxious I became.

Even though we'd learned to tolerate each other, Nick and I were
not friends. But I wanted him home just the same. And more important, I wanted to know he was safe.

The Branch had twisted and manipulated us with the Altered
drug, making us feel a connection to one another that no one else
could ever understand. They'd wanted to create a perfect, cohesive
unit that listened to their programmed commander without question.

I'd been the programmed commander, and the boys had listened
to me without fail, even when they didn't want to, which was especially true for Nick.

We'd been testing ourselves for weeks now, trying to document the exact moment the programming wore off. Nick had been the most eager. He just wanted to be done with it.

Every Wednesday morning, we went out in the backyard and we tested two things: the boys' ability to ignore my orders and their ability to stay put even when they thought I was in danger.

Those were two of the main components of the Altered drug. The boys had felt an undeniable, inexplicable need to protect me—the drug's built-in backup. The Branch wanted to be sure that the boys wouldn't turn on me even if they found out what was going on.

We knew from Sam's more frequent flashbacks that he was most likely the least affected by the drug, so we tested him first. And when I'd given him an order, he'd just stared at me.

Then I pointed a gun at my head.

Cas reacted first. He swept my feet out from underneath me and grabbed my wrist, shoving the gun away. Nick was there a second later, catching me before I hit the ground.

Sam hadn't moved.

Cas and Nick, those first few weeks, listened to every single order I gave them. Hop on one foot. Bawk like a chicken. Nick loved that one.

By the third week, Cas no longer had to obey me.

By the fourth week, *Sam* had pointed a gun at my head, and Nick had slammed him to the ground.

The fifth week, Nick refused to do any more testing.

So that was my excuse, I decided. The whole reason I wanted to know Nick was safe. Because we were somehow still connected through the Altered drug. There was no proof that our link to each other had worn off like with Cas and Sam.

And if that wasn't the reason, I had no idea what was.

When Sam wasn't training me for one thing or another, I usually did an hour or two's worth of research on the flash drive Trev had given us when we'd escaped the Branch. He'd stolen the files as a way to say he was sorry, but it could never make up for betraying us, for picking the Branch over me when I'd needed him.

At the head of the kitchen table, laptop open in front of me, I clicked through the main file labeled ANNA O'BRIEN. There were at least a half-dozen subfolders, some of which I'd yet to fully explore. Today I was on a mission, so I opened the O'BRIEN FAMILY folder and started skimming.

I was determined to convince Sam that learning more about my family could be important for both of us. After all, our pasts were connected to Dani, and I thought it was worthwhile to know her story in order to move forward with our future.

And, more than anything, I wanted to know my older sister, even if I learned about her indirectly. I'd take whatever I could get.

Dani had been part of the Branch long before me. She, Nick, and Cas were to join Sam as the first candidates in the Branch's genetic

alteration program. Once the Branch was successful with the alterations, they'd turned the boys into assassins. They even had résumés
with lists of successful kills, from a U.S. senator to a scientist to a for-
eign diplomat.

Although I knew what Sam and the others were capable of, I still
had a hard time connecting the Sam I knew now to the Sam who'd
spent his days planning missions and following through with kill
orders.

It was even harder to imagine my older sister doing the same
thing, though we'd been unable to find anything that said she'd ever
been an assassin. But if she hadn't, what role had she played in the
Branch?

I'd read her files over and over again and come away with nothing
important. But that didn't mean there weren't clues present, something between the lines.

I decided to start over.

Dani O'Brien: Entered Branch March 12. Moved to Cam
Marie for initial treatments. Will be integrated into unit #1
May 22.

April 28: Dani has responded well to treatments. OB has
requested a shift in the time line. Dani will be introduced to
unit #1 this afternoon.

April 29: Dani's introduction to unit #1 a success. All
accepted her.

May 2: Dani shows successful signs of heightened senses,
greater strength, and a slower rate of aging.

I skimmed the rest of the page, then opened the picture attached to the file. It was of Dani standing in front of a white brick wall, hair hanging loose around her shoulders. It looked like an ID picture, one you'd put on a company badge.

While she wasn't exactly smiling, she didn't look sad. She looked hopeful. There was a glow to her cheeks, a brightness in her eyes.

It was a far departure from the few minor flashbacks I'd had of her. In every memory, she was unkempt, disheveled, worn-out. In the picture, it was as if she was about to embark on a new adventure and couldn't wait to get started.

I opened a new file, this one labeled WILLIAM O'BRIEN. Will was my biological father's older brother. From what I could tell, he'd been close to our family. The picture of him looked like it'd been taken covertly. In it, he was crossing the street in some nondescript town, dark sunglasses hiding his eyes.

His hair was the color of cinnamon, like Dani's, kept short and neatly trimmed. Freckles covered his face.

Based on what little information I'd been able to find, he was still alive. But he had vanished off the face of the earth over six years ago. I couldn't dig up anything on him, not even a parking ticket, which made me wonder if he knew about the Branch and how it had ruined our family, and if he'd been in hiding ever since. I wasn't giving up hope that he was out there somewhere. I'd find him eventually. He might have answers to my past that no one else did.

A coffee mug was thrust in front of me. I looked over my shoulder

at Sam. He was freshly shaven, dark hair still glistening from the
shower.

"Hey," I said, taking the mug in my hands. The coffee inside was
such a light brown, one might argue it was more milk than coffee, but
that's the way I liked it. And I liked it even more that Sam knew that.

"Hey," he answered. "Have you eaten yet?"

No. "Yes."

"She's lying," Cas called from the laundry room. I hadn't even
known he was there.

"How would you know?"

Cas came into the kitchen as he shrugged into a navy-blue flannel
shirt. "Because if you had cooked something, I would have smelled it,
obviously."

I checked the clock on the laptop. It was close to noon. "Fine. I'll
make something now. I have everything for spaghetti and—"

The front door burst open.

Cas and Sam armed themselves and pressed into the wall that
backed up against the living room.

I hid beside an old rickety buffet and mentally calculated the feet
between me and the closest gun in the house. There was one in the
laundry room, hidden in an old box of powdered laundry detergent.

Ten feet, give or take.

I could reach it.

"It's just me, dumbasses," someone called.

Nick.

I came out of my hiding spot and headed for the front of the house.

Cas was just tossing aside a flashlight when I walked in.

"What did you plan on using that for?" Nick said. "Were you going to blind me to death?"

Cas picked the flashlight up again. "Would you like a demonstration?" He cocked it over his shoulder. "Bet I can brain you faster than you can punch me."

Nick's shoulders rocked back. He tightened his jaw as if he were trying to decide which was more important—besting Cas or looking like the mature one who wouldn't take the bait.

"Bet you can't," he finally said, and Cas grinned.

"Stop it," Sam said. He wrenched the flashlight out of Cas's hand.

"Come on!" Cas whirled around. "I had it in the bag!"

"Like we need to be dealing with a concussion right now." Sam set the flashlight upright on the fireplace mantel. He nodded at Nick. "You get the space you needed?"

"I guess." Nick dropped onto the corner of the couch. "I came home earlier than I wanted."

Sam, face blank, voice even, said, "No one forced you."

"No." Nick scrubbed at his face, then said, "Sit down. We need to talk."

Sam pulled himself straighter, suddenly on alert. "About what?"

Cas sauntered over to the second chair and sat down. I sat on the other end of the couch.

"I went out last night with the girl who works at the grocery store in Millerton," Nick said, looking at me. "Remember, the dark-haired girl?"

"How could I forget?"

He ignored me. "We were talking this morning, and she ended up telling me that someone came into the store asking for Anna."

I sat forward. "What do you mean, asking for me?"

"Asking if anyone had seen you. They knew your name. Had an outdated picture of you."

Sam paced in front of the fireplace, arms crossed over his chest. "Did the girl have a description of whoever was doing the asking?"

Nick nodded. His expression was pinched, stressed at the eyes, as if he already had a theory as to who it was. "Girl our age. Reddish-brown hair. Skinny. Five-seven or so."

"Branch agent?" I said.

The boys were silent.

Sam was the first one to speak. "A Branch agent wouldn't be dumb enough to ask about us in a grocery store. They would know it'd tip us off if word got around, and asking about a missing girl in a place like this—small town, safe—it'd turn into a local story by week's end."

"It was a message," Nick said.

I frowned. "Who would it be, though? If not a Branch agent?"

Cas cleared his throat, which was his way of warning me that what he was about to say wouldn't be good. "We know only one girl our age with reddish-brown hair who would be asking for you, Banana."

Nick and Sam shared a look. Sam gave the barest of nods.

"Who?"

"Dani," Sam said.

My first instinct was to laugh, but it clearly wasn't meant as a joke. All three of them were staring at me, tense, waiting for my response.

"No," I said quickly, matter-of-factly. "Dani is dead."

"Says the Branch," Sam said.

"And *they're* trustworthy," Nick added sarcastically.

"It could be anyone. *Anyone.* Someone who used to work for the Branch. Someone who knows Trev." I felt like I was sputtering, making up excuses. It couldn't be Dani.

There wasn't even a tiny part of me that believed it.

"That store in Millerton, it have a security system? Cameras?" Sam asked.

"Yeah," Nick and I said in unison.

Sam gestured to Nick. Nick stood up.

"Wait," I said. "What are you going to do?"

"Look at the tapes." Sam pulled on his coat. "See who it was."

"I'm coming with."

He checked the magazine in his gun, making sure it was full. "No, you're not. If someone was there asking for you, then you're at a greater risk than any of us."

"How are you going to access the security footage?"

Sam gave me a look from under the heavy furrow of his brow, like that was the silliest question I'd ever asked and no way was he going to answer it.

"It'd be far easier to ask to see it, don't you think?" I said. "Instead of sneaking in?"

"Because I'm sure they let any customer who walks in the door access their security system?"

"Let me come," I said. "I have an idea, but you'll need me there to do it."

"Anna." Sam sighed.

Cas walked up behind me. "Oh, let her come, Sammy. She might be useful."

I wasn't sure if I should thank Cas or scowl at him.

"Fine," Sam said. "But if there is any sign of trouble, you leave. Right away. No questions asked."

I nodded. "Fair enough."

He started for the door. "And make sure you have a gun on you."

Worried that he'd leave without me if he had the chance, I grabbed the closest gun—the one from the laundry room—and hurried after him.

6

TREV ONCE TOLD ME THE ART TO LYING
was in telling as much of the truth as you could.

"I lost touch with my sister a long time ago," I said to the grocery store manager. "And your store clerk said there was a girl here the other day asking about me, and it sounds like she fits my sister's description." I wrung my hands in front of me, trying to act as desperate as I could. "Is there any way you could show us the security footage from that day? Just so I could see if it was her?"

The manager, a woman in her forties with long black hair and wide brown eyes, looked from me to Sam, who stood just over my shoulder. Per the plan, Sam had come with me posing as my boyfriend, while Nick stayed in the car on lookout and Cas sauntered around the store.

"I don't know," the woman said. Her name tag read MARGARET, but I thought she looked more like a Maggie.

I sensed her wavering, so I charged on. "Please? I miss her so much." I let my voice hitch at the end, my eyes water.

Her keys jangled in her hand. "All right. I suppose we're not hurting anything. Follow me."

She led us through an unlabeled door near the front of the store, just past the checkout lines. On the other side was a small office. There, two black-and-white TVs played security footage from several cameras spread around the store.

Margaret took a seat at the desk and unlocked the lone computer. "Do you know what day it was that your sister supposedly came in?"

"Thursday," I answered.

Sam hovered near the desk, arms crossed in front of him. I could just make out the shape of his gun holster slung over his shoulders, hidden beneath his jacket. Before all of this, when I was just a normal girl living a semi-abnormal life, seeing someone with a gun always made me nervous. Riley, the Branch's second-in-command and the one who usually made the checkup visits to the lab, carried a gun with him at all times. Maybe that was why I'd avoided him. Well, that among other things. He was a weaselly, unpleasant person who'd do anything for the Branch. He didn't question what the entity did and how they did it, which made him that much more dangerous to us.

I was glad for the gun now strapped to *my* shoulders. Going anywhere without it would've left me feeling vulnerable and naked. We'd learned that Riley had the unfortunate ability to pop up at any time.

Margaret queued the footage from Thursday and fast-forwarded through the afternoon, starting at one o'clock, when Nick's "friend" had been working. Several people came and went through the check-out lanes. The time readout on the screen said over an hour had passed on the footage.

And then, finally, we found what we were looking for.

"Wait. Go back," I said. A girl fitting the description Nick relayed had come and gone on the footage. I'd seen only a flash of her face, but it was enough to put me instantly on alert. Trepidation crept up my spine. "Can you play it here?"

Margaret pressed a button and the footage slowed to real time.

The girl came through the checkout lane, long hair loose down her back. She faced away from the camera at first and handed something to the clerk. A picture, I thought.

The clerk scanned it and nodded quickly before handing the picture back.

After a few more words were exchanged between the two, the girl finally turned toward the exit, toward the camera.

A startled breath rushed down my throat.

"Shit," Sam said.

I blinked back the sudden welling of tears and covered my mouth with my hand to stop the choked sound of surprise threatening to escape me.

Dani.

It was her.

Margaret glanced over a shoulder, a smile spread across her face. "Is that your sister?"

The reply to that question was just one word, easy enough to say but impossible to get out. Because saying it brought her back from the dead. Saying it meant I was no longer the last remaining member of my family.

I wanted it to be true more than anything, but after what I'd been through in the last few months, the cautious, rational side of me said don't believe it just yet. This could be another trap. Another lie told by the Branch. They were capable of anything. Had the security feed been tampered with? Had they somehow added Dani's image to the footage?

I couldn't allow myself to give in to the hope.

"I can ask my employee if the girl left any contact information," Margaret said.

Sam gestured to the screen. "You got cameras on the parking lot?"

Margaret frowned. "Well, yes, but..."

"Bring it up, please? Find the time stamp for directly after this one here, with the clerk."

"All right." Margaret typed in a few commands, and new footage replaced the interior shots. Dani emerged from the store, crossed the parking lot, and started for the alley. So she wasn't driving. Or if she was, she'd parked out of sight.

"Should I rewind it?" Margaret asked and moved to type in another command when Sam stopped her.

"Wait."

A black sedan pulled up behind Dani. The taillights glowed red against the slushy asphalt. Someone got out from the passenger side.

Dani kept walking, hands shoved in the pockets of her coat. Did she know someone was behind her?

The man pulled a gun from a hidden shoulder holster.

"Oh my God," Margaret said.

Dani whipped around.

The man didn't have enough time to react, and Dani caught him in the nose with a left-handed punch. He spun back, facing the camera.

Even in the static of an old TV screen, I knew the man was Riley. Dread knotted in my gut.

Another agent eased out of the sedan. He came around behind Dani and kicked the back of her knee. She buckled forward. Riley brought down the butt of his gun, catching her across the cheek. Blood poured from her mouth.

Margaret gasped. "We need to call someone," she said, and reached for the phone, knocking over a cup of pens. They rolled off the desk, clattered to the floor. "Oh, that poor girl! I can't believe no one saw it happen. She could be dead by now. . . ."

Sam hit the receiver button. Margaret looked up at him. "What are you doing?"

"Listen very carefully." He gently pulled the receiver from her hand and hung it up. "You can't tell anyone what you just saw."

"But . . . her sister . . ."

Sam set his hands on the arms of her chair and spun her toward him, caging her in place. "That girl isn't her sister," he lied, crafting a tale quickly. "She's a fugitive on the run from the Russian government, and those men are two of their agents. If they know what you saw, they will hurt you and anyone you care about. Do you understand me?"

"What? Are you—"

"Do you understand?" Sam repeated.

Margaret, eyes wider, lips devoid of color, nodded without a sound.

"Erase that footage, got it?" Sam ordered. She didn't move. "Margaret?"

"Yes. Okay." She started tapping randomly at the keyboard. "I can't believe this is happening."

Sam eyed me while he spoke next. "Margaret, we need to go. Are you going to be okay?"

She sniffed, still tapping at the computer. "Yes. I'll be fine. I mean...yes..."

Sam nodded toward the door. I went out ahead of him, and as we left, he whispered, "This is why my way was better."

I couldn't argue with that.

7

WHEN WE REACHED THE CABIN THIRTY
minutes later, we all went our separate ways in a flurry of activity.
Nick was in charge of the laptop and any information we'd printed
off about the Branch. Cas was in charge of the first-aid kit. Sam was
in charge of weapons. I was in charge of the food supply and double-
checking that we didn't leave any clues behind.

"Because you're good at noticing details," Sam had said when
he'd first assigned us to the tasks.

I'd planned ahead, and already had an emergency food supply
bag packed and waiting in the laundry room. I immediately went
upstairs to start checking the house, beginning with Nick's and Cas's
rooms, then the bathroom.

We'd always been good about picking up after ourselves, though

Cas sometimes forgot about the rules or was just too plain lazy to follow them.

The last room on the top floor was the room I shared with Sam. I tore down the three sketches I'd taped on the wall above the bedside table. One was of Cas and Sam playing a game of chess, another of Nick running, and the last one was of Dani. I didn't know when it was in the time line of our life, but it felt like a real memory versus a made-up scene. She was sitting on the floor, holding me in her arms, stroking my hair.

Sometimes when I closed my eyes, I could almost hear her whispering to me.

"Anna?"

I startled at the sound of Sam's voice. "Hey," I said. "I'm almost done."

He nodded and looked at the sketch in my hands. Something guarded crossed his face. Guilt, I thought.

"We're leaving in ten minutes," he said without meeting my eyes, and hurried down the stairs.

I held the sketch up to the light. Sam had never commented on the drawing before. He never talked much about Dani at all, even though I was almost certain he was having more and more flashbacks about her and their life before the Altered program. I wanted him to open up so badly, to know his secrets and his thoughts and worries.

I gently laid the sketches in my journal and slid it into my messenger bag. Next, I checked the dressers, the closet, and the nightstands. Mine was empty, so I went around the bed to Sam's and opened the tiny drawer, crouching to peer inside.

It was bare, as I thought it would be, and I was just about to shut it when I heard the faint scrape of paper against wood.

I looked again but saw nothing, so I pulled the entire drawer out. As I did, a folded piece of paper came with it and dropped to the floor. I set the drawer aside and scooped up the paper. It was a list of names scrawled in pencil in Sam's handwriting. Some had been scribbled over and re-written. Others had asterisks next to them, and some question marks.

Anthony Romna
Joseph Badgley*
~~Sarah T.~~ Sarah Trainor
Edward van der Bleek?

The list went on. It took up the entire page and then some. There had to have been at least thirty names. I scanned all of them to see if I recognized anyone and found two at the bottom. Names I knew well.

Melanie O'Brien?
Charles O'Brien?

My parents.

What were my parents doing on a list of names in Sam's bedside table?

"Yo, Anna!" Cas called.

I flinched and shoved the paper in my back pocket. "Yeah?"

"We're ready, and you haven't even checked the downstairs," Nick yelled.

"I'm coming! Sorry."

Although I was on a completely different floor, I could still hear Nick grumble in response.

I jammed the drawer back in place and hurried downstairs.

When we climbed into the SUV, I looked out the windshield at our third house in two months. I wished I could say I would miss it, but it was hard to grow attached when you knew you were going to be moving soon anyway.

Sam turned on the engine and backed up. Five minutes later, the house was nothing but a speck in the rearview mirror.

"Now what?" Cas asked. "Dani is alive. Riley got her. And they clearly know we're in the area."

"They're using her as bait," Nick said. "They knew we'd see that security footage one way or the other, once we found out someone was asking about Anna."

I twisted around between the front seats. "They couldn't have known you'd go slutting around with the store clerk who just so happened to mention someone was asking about me."

Cas chuckled. "Slutting around. That's funny."

"Either way," Nick went on, teeth gritted, "they knew once you found out your sister was still alive that you'd come looking."

I turned back in my seat. Truth was, I wasn't sure *what* I wanted our next move to be, or whether I wanted to risk our safety in order to go after a sister whom I couldn't remember, who'd supposedly been dead.

How had she survived? Why hadn't she found me before now?

I cringed, recalling the beating she'd suffered at the hands of Riley in the alley behind the grocery store. I could imagine the pain and the fear that'd gone along with it. And if that's what they were willing to do out in public, what they would do to her in private would be so much worse.

"Sam?" I looked over at him. "Weigh in, please?"

He slowed for a stoplight and merged into the left-turn lane, the blinker clicking in the silence of the car. He took a breath. "Nick is right."

"Thank you," Nick said.

"But..." He flicked his attention to me. "She's your sister. If you say you're willing to die to find her, I wouldn't blame you."

Was I?

I wanted to know my family and, in a way, know myself better through them. But the simple fact that Dani was alive when she shouldn't be raised a dozen red flags. Just what was the Branch planning to do with her? Where had she been all this time? And more important, did she know I was with Sam? If she didn't, what would she think about it?

"I guess the first step is finding out where they took her," I said.

Sam made a left turn. Snow and salt thudded against the wheel wells as the car picked up speed.

"Sure, let's do that." Nick cracked a knuckle. "Why don't we just call up Riley and ask where he's storing her?"

"Just say the word," Cas added. "Riley's my bro. I got him on speed dial."

"You're such a dumbass," Nick said.

"Or," Cas said, "we could call Trev. He left us that emergency number on the flash drive. Might as well use it."

Nick snorted. "Further illustrates my point that you're a dumbass."

Sam glanced at me briefly. "You want to go down that road?"

I looked out the passenger-side window. Snow melted on the glass, droplets sliding down. "Trev would probably help us," I said quietly, afraid that if I spoke too loudly, it would somehow not be true. What was he like now, months later? I was afraid to find out. But more than that, I was afraid of him turning us down. If he did, there was no greater proof: He was gone from me for good. The thought left me feeling hollow.

"He'll just set us up again," Nick said.

There was that, too. That was worse than turning us down.

"You don't have to be a part of this," I replied.

I wanted our group to stick together. Strength in numbers and all that. But this was my family we were talking about. If I couldn't save Dani, then I was no better than the Branch. Maybe I wouldn't be the one causing her pain, but was leaving her in their hands when I could save her somehow worse? I couldn't imagine all the things they would do to her in order to find out what she knew.

And, more than anything, I wanted to see her with my own eyes, to see that she was real.

I had a sister out there somewhere. Blood was blood.

I couldn't turn my back on her.

8

I HELD THE PREPAID CELL PHONE IN my hand, staring at the blank screen. Sam sat next to me, Cas across from both of us. We were in a little diner called Elkhorn Original, at a table in the back. All the booths near the windows were open and booths generally gave a person more privacy, but they were also hard to get out of when you were in a hurry. Another Sam lesson.

Nick sat outside on a bench across the street, on point. I couldn't see him, but I trusted he was there. Even though he'd been against this, he was still with the group on most things. Majority vote. We won.

Three mugs of coffee sat on the table between Sam, Cas, and me, but none of us was feeling particularly thirsty. Sam bit into the mint candy he'd been sucking on.

"When he picks up, *if* he picks up," Sam said, "you have two minutes, tops. We don't want to risk being traced. Ask him what you need to ask him, and if he doesn't give you the answer you need, hang up. No hesitation." Sam leaned forward, closer to me. I was still staring at the phone. He set his hand on my knee beneath the table and squeezed.

"It'll be fine," he promised.

When Trev gave us the flash drive, he'd included a document titled IN CASE OF EMERGENCY. It was a text file with a phone number, nothing else. That was the number we were calling now.

I punched it in, brought the phone to my ear. I could barely hear the ringing on the other end over the fierce beating of my heart. Trev had once been my best friend. Talking to him had been easier than talking to anyone else. And now I felt like I might vomit at the thought of hearing his voice. Or maybe it was that I worried it *wouldn't* be him. If the Branch ever found out what he'd given us, they'd either wipe his memory or kill him.

As angry as I was with him, he didn't deserve either of those punishments.

Cas fidgeted across from me and accidentally bumped the table. Coffee sloshed over the rim of his cup and puddled on the table.

"Sorry," he muttered at the same time the line picked up and Trev said, "Hello?"

I looked over at Sam, nodded. He started the timer on his watch. Cas sopped up the coffee mess with a wad of napkins.

"Anna?" Trev said, his voice hitching.

I squeezed my eyes shut. "Yeah. It's me." *Take charge of the conversation. You only have two minutes.* "I need a favor."

He didn't say anything for what felt like much longer than two minutes. Finally, a breath, another pause, then, "What kind of favor?"

"Dani is alive and the Branch has her and I want to know where I might find her."

"What?" There was shuffling through the line, the creak of a door and it closing a second later. "How do you know she's alive?"

"We saw her on the security footage at a grocery store."

"And the Branch, how—"

"They attacked her in the alley there. Riley and another agent."

Trev cursed. Wind whistled through the receiver. There was a dinging noise, like the sound a car made when the door was open. "Give me an hour. You in Michigan?"

Sam shook his head. He must have heard Trev through the line.

"No," I said.

"Sam tell you to say that?" I didn't answer. "Meet me at the wind turbine field in Hart in two hours."

"We are not meeting him," Sam said.

"Anna," Trev said. "Don't use this number again. Okay? It's only good for a one-time use. Meet me. I'll see what I can dig up."

"We are *not* meeting him," Sam repeated. We locked eyes. He shook his head again.

"All right," I said to Trev. "Two hours."

"I'll be there."

The line went dead.

Sam's hands curled into fists. "Damn it, Anna! We are not meeting him."

"That's fine." I stood. "You don't have to. Just like I told Nick: I can do this alone."

Sam rose to his feet next to me. There were only two inches between us. I could smell the leftover mint on his breath, could practically feel the heat in his voice. "You really think we'd let you go alone?"

No. I didn't. Which was why I was making a stand now. I needed this, and I was willing to risk a lot to get it.

"I don't know," I answered. "Maybe."

Cas snorted. "She's totally baiting us."

The corners of Sam's eyes pinched tighter. He knew it, too. "Fine," he said. "Since this is your mission, I'll let you brief Nick."

He turned and walked out the door. I watched him go. Across from me, Cas practically vibrated with laughter. "Nick is going to love this plan."

I grumbled to myself as I plodded outside.

Nick took the news like we all thought he would, with an air of disgruntled arrogance. He now sat in the backseat, silent as we headed for Hart, Michigan. The GPS said we were over two hours out, but Sam kept the speedometer just above seventy-five the whole way there. Thankfully the freeways were clear of snow and ice, otherwise we'd be late.

We could see the wind turbines long before we reached our destination. The blades rose above the bare, gray treetops. There had to be four dozen of them, total, dotted here and there across the skyline.

When we pulled into the field, the turbines towered over us. It was hard not to feel small and insignificant next to them. The dirt road curved through the field. We could see straight back to the line of pine trees, so we were easily able to spot Trev's car. It was parked on the access road to the sixth turbine. It was a brand-new luxury sedan with tinted windows and chrome wheels and a shiny jaguar hood ornament.

Trev was leaning against the passenger side.

The moment we were close enough to recognize him, my stomach turned itself into knots. I was ridiculously happy to see him, but that feeling was mixed with the sudden overwhelming need to double-check that my gun was in place.

My mind didn't want to trust him. My heart did.

When we pulled in, Sam whipped a quick U-turn so that the car faced the exit.

I got out before Sam could tell me all the things I should or shouldn't do.

The snow and gravel crunched beneath my boots. Trev took a step away from the car, a manila envelope tucked beneath his arm.

The boys were out of the vehicle in a matter of seconds, guns at their sides.

"Stop it, you guys," I said.

I looked over the fifteen feet that separated me from Trev. He looked good. Black dress pants matched a black suit jacket partially hidden beneath a black trench. A gray scarf was tied around his neck, and his hands were covered in black leather gloves. His shoes were leather, too, narrow, almost pointed, at the toes.

I don't know what I expected, but it wasn't this. I expected him to be in jeans. I expected him to look sad. I expected him not to be dressed in expensive clothes, driving an expensive car, with his black hair slicked back.

I expected him to still look like Trev.

"Hey," I said.

"Hey."

There was a long, awkward pause.

Trev was the first one to break the silence, and he jumped right into business mode. "I was able to dig up some locations that might be useful. I found no mention of Dani's intake. I couldn't verify that she was at any Branch location, but if she was, I'd guess it'd be a lab." He tapped the edge of the manila envelope against the palm of his glove and looked away, his breath punctuating the air around him. "It's good to see you, Anna."

I took three steps closer. Slow, deliberate steps, like I was approaching an old family pet that may or may not have contracted rabies. "You look different."

He pointed the envelope my way. "So do you."

"Not as different as you."

He glanced down. "Yeah, well...I don't have any good response to that."

I crossed my arms over my chest. "I don't get one of your memorized literary quotes? Nothing to put me at ease?"

He licked his lips. "Would it help?"

"Probably not."

He nodded. A ghost of a smile touched the corners of his mouth, but then he glanced over my shoulder, and the smile faded.

Nick marched forward. "We've already been here too long. Give me the damn envelope so we can be on our way." Nick stopped two feet from Trev, hand extended.

Trev narrowed his eyes. "Anna asked for the info. Anna is the one I give it to."

I didn't have to see Nick's face to know there was a snarl on his lips. "Give me the goddamn envelope."

"I see you're still as much a dickhead as you were two months ago," Trev answered.

Nick struck first, but Trev was already ducking out of the way. He grabbed Nick's wrist as he twisted around and flipped Nick over his shoulders. Nick landed with a heavy *thud* on the snow-covered, frozen dirt.

Trev didn't waste a second. He scrambled on top of Nick, jammed a knee in Nick's chest, and pulled a gun from a hidden shoulder holster.

He pointed the gun at Nick's head.

"Put it down," Sam said. He edged around me, his gun aimed at Trev. Cas came from the other side. His gun was out, too.

I hadn't reacted at all. Trev had always been the quiet one, the smart one, the one who fought more with words than hands. Either he'd learned a lot in the last two months with the Branch, or he'd kept more secrets from us than just his identity.

"We're not on the same team anymore, I get it," Trev said, the gun still trained on Nick even though he was addressing Sam. "That also means I don't have to put up with his vitriol, either."

Cas snickered. "I don't think Nick knows what *vitriol* means."

"Get. Off. Me," Nick said, his teeth clenched tightly.

Trev eased away, slid the gun back in its holster. He straightened the flap of his trench coat, hiding the gun once again.

I plucked the envelope from the ground, where it'd been dropped. I bent the metal clips, tugged the flap open. There was a thin stack of papers inside, stapled together.

"You'll find the name of the lab and the address," Trev explained. "I also included blueprints, so you can plan for blind spots."

Sam came up behind me and read over my shoulder.

"All of the labs were given Greek alphabet names," Trev went on. "Ours was the Alpha lab. Beta lab was shut down before we even got out. Something wrong with the treatments. They hadn't perfected an Altered drug that would work in any group besides ours."

"You keep saying 'ours' like there ever was an 'ours,'" Sam said.

Trev fixed his hair. "Fine. You. Your group. Kappa lab barely got off the ground before there was an incident."

"What kind of incident?" I asked.

Trev shook his head. "I'm not telling you that." He didn't wait for me to argue before continuing. "There's only one lab still up and running today: Delta. If Dani is anywhere, I'd guess it'd be there."

"Do you know for sure she's not at headquarters?"

He nodded. "I was just there yesterday. If she were there, I would have known it."

"Why, you Riley's right-hand man now?" Nick asked.

Trev looked like he wanted to roll his eyes but didn't. "No. I'm the head of the intake department."

I felt the urge to gape but buried it quickly. "Head of the department?"

"Just the intake department," he repeated, like that somehow lessened the admission.

"Does Riley know you gave us the flash drive?"

"No."

"Doesn't he suspect you at all? I mean…you lived with us for over five years. You…" I trailed off, because I wasn't sure what else to say that wouldn't sound pathetic.

Trev just stared at me, the space between his brows pulled tight with apologies and regret.

Wind rushed through the field. The blades of the turbines picked up speed.

Whump whump whump.

I shivered. "We have to go."

He nodded. "I know."

I turned for the vehicle. Sam was already there, holding the door open for me. Nick and Cas trailed behind, putting themselves between Trev and me.

"Anna?" Trev called. I stopped and glanced over my shoulder. I braced myself for one of his quotes. I wanted to hear one. Something to tell me that a part of the Trev I knew was still there, hidden somewhere in that expensive suit and tailored trench coat.

But all he said was, "I hope you find her," before climbing into his car.

9

SINCE WE WERE WITHOUT A SAFE LOCA-
tion, we headed to the next best thing: an IHOP. Chain restaurants
were good for safety and coverage. They were usually busy, so it was
easy to blend in. At the same time, it was hard for anyone to attack,
because there were so many witnesses.

Cas and Nick sat across from Sam and me. Cas had ordered the
biggest meal he possibly could, to keep up his strength, according to
him. It included eggs and bacon and toast and hash browns and pancakes. The rest of us stuck with the basics. For me, that was just a
cheese omelet. But I wasn't feeling very hungry.

Nick leaned across the table, keeping his voice low. While being
in a public place afforded us safety and anonymity, it also gave us very
little privacy. "Do I even have to say it? Trusting Trev is a bad idea."

I stared at the gap between Cas and Nick, vision blurred, thinking. The part of me more concerned with self-preservation agreed with Nick. I'd never tell him that, of course. But meeting Trev, trusting his information, it was all a huge risk. And if I pursued this, the boys would follow. There was no doubt in my mind about that. Which meant this wasn't just about me. If I got caught while looking for my sister, they would get caught, too.

"Imagine if it was someone you cared about," Cas said. "You'd do anything for them, right?"

Nick snorted. "That's why I don't care about anyone."

"I trust him," I said suddenly, blinking. "Trev has had more than one opportunity to turn us in. He's had more than one opportunity to kill us, if that's what he wanted. But he hasn't. If he was truly one hundred percent with the Branch, we wouldn't be having this conversation right now. We would have been surrounded by agents in that turbine field."

Sam took a drink of his coffee, his fingers curled around the rim of the mug. When he set the cup down, he slouched in his chair and extended his arm across the back of my chair. "She's right. The Branch had no reason to draw this out. If they wanted us, they would have had us by now. Trev had the opportunity. I say we check out the lab. There could be others like us." He flicked his attention across the table, eyeing Cas and Nick. The boys had always had some kind of connection that allowed them to communicate silently with nothing but a look or a blink or a twitch of the mouth. I imagined it was something they'd learned from their time as trained assassins, back before the farmhouse lab.

Cas cleared his plate, wiped his mouth with the napkin before tossing it to the table. "It's been months since I've done any ass kicking. I'm dying to get some action."

"I bet you are," Nick muttered. "But you might have to beg for it."

Cas grinned. "Good one, Nicky poo."

Sam's hand trailed down along my spine before coming to a stop at the small of my back. I twisted his way, our knees bumping beneath the table.

"You sure about this?" he asked.

I nodded. "As sure as I'll ever be."

"Then we should get going." He gestured to the manila envelope tucked in my bag. "Delta lab is several hours off. If we get on the road now, we should reach it before dawn."

The boys pushed back their chairs to leave.

"Wait," I said. "Can I call my dad before we leave?"

It'd been over two weeks since I'd spoken to him. Our relationship wasn't perfect, not now, not in the past. And even though he'd lied to me for over five years and posed as my father while he led the farmhouse Altered program, I still felt like he was family. He'd helped us escape when we'd needed him and he'd stood behind us at Branch headquarters. He'd even taken a bullet to save me.

"Use the oldest prepaid," Sam said. "We'll meet you outside in ten minutes."

"Ten minutes," I agreed.

They filed toward the door. "Anna?" Sam called over a shoulder. "Don't tell him where we're going."

"I won't."

Hearing my dad's voice always made me feel instantly at home, like we were back at the old farmhouse in New York, discussing the news over dinner. Back when everything was normal, at least for us. When we were safe.

"Anna," Dad said when he realized it was me. "It's good to hear from you. Everything all right?"

I held the phone tighter. "Yeah. Everything's fine. Just thought I'd check in with you."

He sighed. "Everything is *not* all right, is it?"

All the tension ran out of my shoulders, and I slouched in my seat. My dad and I had never been close, even when we'd lived in the same house, when I'd thought the life I had was the truth. But if there was one thing my dad was good at, it was knowing a lie when he heard it.

"When will anything ever be all right?" I laughed to lighten the mood. "That's not why I'm calling, though. I really just called to talk to you. How have you been?"

"Well... I'm still having trouble sleeping at night, but that's to be expected. Everything has healed well enough. I'm just old." He chuckled and it turned into a drawn-out hacking fit. "Sorry," he said, once he'd recovered. "It's this dry air."

Somehow I didn't think it was the air. I ran my finger through salt left on the table. The grains stuck to my skin.

"So, how are the boys?" Dad asked.

I looked out the restaurant's windows to the parking lot beyond. I could just make out the roof of our SUV and the heads of the boys lined up alongside it, waiting. "The same, I guess. Cas won't stop eating. Nick won't stop being a jerk. And Sam..." I trailed off, because while my dad wasn't technically my *biological* dad, he was still the closest thing I had to one. Heat burned through my cheeks. Sam was a subject I didn't feel comfortable elaborating on. "Sam is good," I finished.

"Have you had any run-ins with the Branch?"

"No, but..."

"But what?"

"Did you know there were other labs?"

There was a rustle through the line as Dad shifted. I imagined him reaching for a straw to chew on. It'd been his habit for nearly four years. Ever since he gave up smoking. "I didn't know for sure, but I always imagined there were. That's what their goal was, to make more kids like you."

"How many more?"

"I don't know."

I checked the clock above the front counter. My ten minutes were nearly up.

"You aren't going after them, are you?" Dad asked. "Trying to play the vigilante, save the others like you?"

"No," I said, because that was the truth. At least, that wasn't our first goal. Finding Dani was. Saving the others, if there were others, would just be a bonus.

"If not that, then what? Why ask about the other labs now?"

I wanted so badly to tell him about my sister. I wanted to tell someone. But Sam would be furious, and involving my dad would only put him in danger.

"I can't tell you the details. You know that."

He sighed. "Yes. I know."

"My time is up."

"All right." He pulled in a breath. "Just be careful, all right? Please?"

"We always are."

"I meant you, Anna."

I gritted my teeth against the sudden burning in my eyes. "I will."

We said our good-byes and I hung up the phone. The prepaid was no longer good, as far as Sam was concerned, so I tossed it into what remained of my iced tea and hurried to the door. I wanted to reach Delta lab as soon as possible, before Riley or anyone else did something terrible to my sister and she ended up dead all over again.

10

THE ADDRESS FOR DELTA LAB WAS IN the middle of Indiana. Sam followed the GPS directions till we were two miles outside the lab's location and then turned onto a long, winding driveway that circled an abandoned textile factory. He parked behind the building. "Let's travel on foot from here," he said.

As Sam, Cas, and Nick went around to the back to load themselves with weapons, I shrugged out of my coat and draped it across the passenger seat so I could slip into a shoulder holster.

Next, I checked the clip in my gun, making sure it was full before sliding it into place at my side. I put my coat on again, leaving it unzipped.

"Ready?" Sam asked around the side of the vehicle.

I tugged my knit hat down low. The air was freezing, and already my ears were numb. Running would help, at least, and I was looking forward to it. "I'm ready."

Cas rounded the front of the vehicle, his boots crunching in the snow. "Ready, boss."

"Ready," Nick said.

We headed into the woods.

———

Months ago, I'd barely been able to keep up with Sam when it came to running. Since then, I'd taken the once-optional sport more seriously and tried to run daily. Still, Sam was faster than I was, and he'd already pulled ahead.

I counted my breaths the way he'd taught me. One, two, three, four. One, two, three, four. It was all about finding a place, a focus point straight ahead. And I'd learned I could go a lot longer and a lot harder than I'd thought I could. My body wouldn't give out on me after ten minutes, despite my doubts.

We spread out in a V, with Cas and Nick on Sam's left, me on the right. I was almost keeping pace with Cas. We ran silently, like ghosts. A sense of strength and power poured through me, and my breathing evened out.

When the trees thinned, we slowed and cut through a grove of pines—the only trees in the forest that would afford us some cover this time of year.

A house came into view.

It was a sprawling estate positioned at the top of a hill that over-looked a river. A massive deck hung over the hill, but was empty of everything, including lawn furniture. There were no lights on inside.

"What do you think?" Cas whispered.

"Looks deserted," I answered.

"Cas and Nick, around front," Sam said. "Look for their handler. Anna, with me."

Nick and Cas nodded and disappeared.

"We're going up the north end," Sam said to me. "To the base-ment entrance below the deck."

According to the blueprint Trev had given us, the lab was in the basement, fifteen feet from the entrance door.

Sam motioned me forward, and we jogged up the hill, ducking beneath the deck. Sam pressed his back against the house's exterior wall, on the right side of the entrance. I echoed his movements, tak-ing the left side, pulling my gun out as the cold of the brick founda-tion seeped through my jacket.

Sam inched forward and twisted the metal doorknob. The door opened, the thick weather stripping expanding with a sigh. Sam froze. I counted to ten. Nothing. No one moved on the other side. No alarms went off. No lights clicked on.

We slipped inside and entered into what might have once been a mudroom. Empty hooks dotted the wall across from us. Below them sat a bench. A few logs were stacked on end in a tin bucket near the door. The air smelled faintly of burning wood and ash.

I craned my neck, checking the hallway straight ahead, gun up, ready. A thick steel door stood at the end. A keypad was installed in the wall to the right.

The lab was exactly where the blueprints had said it'd be.

Sam gestured to the rest of the basement, meaning we should finish our check first.

The basement wasn't large, so it took us only a few minutes to be sure we were alone. Sam was the first to the lab door. I hovered behind him as he inspected the keypad.

"I don't know if I'll be able to break into this," he said quietly. "It's high-tech, more advanced than the system at the farmhouse."

"So what do we do?"

"We hope Cas and Nick find the handler, and the handler gives us the code."

I snorted. "Like he's going to give that up?"

"I can be convincing," he said without looking at me.

"What, and torture him? You can't. If the handler is anything at all like my dad—"

"You want your sister, don't you?" He finally met my eyes. "How else are we going to get inside? Call Riley direct and see if he knows the code?"

"You don't have to be a jerk."

"I'm not, I'm just trying to—"

A door clicked open somewhere above us. Clean white light spilled down the stairwell. I tightened my hold on my gun.

"It's us," Cas said. "We found the handler."

I exhaled and followed Sam around to the staircase. Nick was dragging a man down the stairs. Cas led the way. The man nearly stumbled over the last two steps, and Nick had to catch him beneath the arms to steady him.

"Take whatever you want," the man said, his voice hitching with panic. "My wallet is upstairs. I don't know how much cash I have, but I have credit cards and—"

"We're not here for your money," Sam said.

I stepped around Sam to get a better look at the Delta lab handler. He was nothing like my dad.

He was younger, for one. Thirties, maybe, with a full head of dirty-blond hair and a neatly trimmed goatee. A tie hung loose from around his neck. The first three buttons of his white oxford were undone.

"Open the lab," Sam said.

The edge of distress on the man's face disappeared, replaced with curiosity and caution. "You're him, aren't you?"

Sam didn't even blink.

"Sam. And…" The man examined the rest of us. "Cas. Nick. And…" His attention landed on me. "Anna."

"So we can skip the introductions," Nick said, giving the man a tug. "Now open the lab."

"I can't. You know what they'd do to me if I did?"

Nick kicked the man behind the knee. He wailed and dropped to the floor. Nick twisted his arms higher, pushing the sockets of his shoulders as far as they would go before dislocating.

"You have any idea what *we* will do to you if you don't open that lab?" Nick said.

The man started sobbing. "Please don't hurt me. I'm just a scientist. I run the logs and the tests. That's it."

Nick pushed the man's arms higher. "Then open the door."

He cried out. "Okay! Okay! Stop. Please."

Nick looked up at Sam. Sam nodded and Nick let the man go. He cowered on the floor for several long seconds holding his arms close to his chest.

Get up, I thought, *before Nick or Sam does something worse.*

I couldn't help but see my dad in this man's place. Even if he worked for the Branch, I wasn't sure he deserved to be tortured.

Finally, he crawled to his knees, then used the wall for support as he stood up. He shuffled toward the lab, the rest of us trailing behind.

He punched in the code, and the door hissed open.

Nick went in first, gun at the ready. Sam nudged the man inside. Cas and I followed.

The lab was dark. I could only make out the shape of the cells straight ahead, so I tried to focus on all the things Sam had taught me in the last few weeks: *What do you smell? What do you feel? Don't tense up. Keep your finger near the trigger of the gun, but not on it, not till you're ready to shoot. Listen to your gut; it'll always be right.*

But even with his advice running through my head, I couldn't focus on any of those things as the lab widened before me. It was like I was home again, like Dad was to my right working at his desk, chewed-up straws piled around him. Cas in the cell farthest to the left. His room full of junk. Nick all the way to the right, ignoring me. Trev next to Cas, in his room reading. Sam, at the glass wall, watching.

My throat closed around a lump.

If we found Dani here, what would happen between Sam and me? The thought hit me square in the chest, till I felt like I couldn't breathe. I'd been so concerned with my past and my family, and saving the one member I might have left, that I'd forgotten to consider what might happen when Sam saw Dani again.

"Turn on the lights," Nick ordered.

The man went to the control panel and hit a button. The ceiling lights flickered on.

Unlike the lab at our farmhouse, which had only four cells, this one had six. And there were boys in at least two of them. They stood at the front of their rooms, in the same Branch-issued gray cotton pants and white cotton shirts that the boys had worn all those years.

They were just like us.

I scanned the remaining cells, looking for Dani. The other rooms were dark.

"Is there a girl here?" I crossed the lab to the control panel. "Reddish hair? Beaten, maybe. Dani. Is Dani here?"

The man shook his head, eyes wide, hands held up in front of him. I looked down at the gun still in my hands, the barrel pointed at the man's chest. I pulled it away.

"You're sure?"

"I don't have any Danis here," he answered.

"But do you have any girls?"

"Um." He licked his lips. "There's a—"

A floorboard creaked from somewhere beyond the lab. All four of us froze. Sam gestured to Cas and Nick, then pointed to the left side of the mouth of the hallway. They took their positions and Sam went to the opposite side.

I slid in beside him. Footsteps edged nearer. I closed my eyes, listened. One set of steps. Another. Another. And finally, a fourth. The person at the front of the pack shifted, and I caught the faint sound of metal rattling. A gun. They came forward, one slow, agonizing step at a time. It was the gun that entered the lab first.

Sam grabbed the gun barrel first and pushed up and clocked the person—a man—across the jaw with a left-handed punch. The gun dropped to the floor with a clatter as Sam swung the man around, tossing him into the front wall of the third cell. The thick glass vibrated from the hit, and the boy inside stepped back.

Cas lunged at the next person to enter the lab. A woman, dressed in black combat gear—thick pants, boots tied at her calves, rubber padding on the shoulders and elbows of a thick black jacket, bulletproof vest.

Agents.

Cas punched her in the face. The woman went straight down, knocked out.

Nick went after the third agent. I went after the fourth.

I threw a knee into the man's groin, then drove another up into his chin. When I gave him a shove, he slumped to the floor, unconscious. I breathed out, the gun still in my left hand.

A fifth agent dropped me with a swipe of his foot. I landed on my back, and my spine seized. My gun skittered away. The agent grabbed one of my feet and yanked me toward the door. The rough concrete tore the skin on my palms as I struggled to grab hold of something.

The man dragged me into the main part of the basement and tossed me against the wall. I hit the edge of the bench as I came down, knocking it and the tin bucket over. The logs spilled every which way. I snatched one up, swung. The agent ducked. I swung again, grazing the top of his head, and when I came back for another hit, he threw a blow to my gut.

The air rushed out of me. I doubled over. The man tore the log from my hand, raised it over his shoulder as if he meant to hit me with it. I braced myself for the impact as a shot rang out.

A bullet wound appeared in the man's chest, and when he fell over, I saw Sam standing just a few feet away, lowering his gun.

"Thank you," I started as the door burst open behind me.

"Go!" Sam yelled, motioning me toward the stairs.

"I'm not leaving you!"

Agents filled the room. I had no gun. No weapon at all.

"Damn it, Anna!" Sam yelled, tossing me his gun as an agent rushed toward him. Sam stomped at an angle with his boot, and the agent's ankle snapped. He slammed down to one knee, and Sam punched the man in the back of the head. The man pitched forward.

I snatched the gun easily from the air, pointed, shot. Another agent down with a bullet hole in his knee. I sighted a dark-haired man as Cas appeared next to me, shooting two agents with a quick squeeze of the trigger.

I shot until my clip ran empty.

"Sam!" I called. He tossed me a full magazine without question, and I slammed it into place, taking out another agent before he could get close.

Cas turned to me, a grin spread across his face. But it slipped away quickly and he brought his gun up, pointing it right at me as an arm wrapped around my throat and dragged me back. Cas was too distracted to see the dark-haired woman come up behind him. She kicked him in the kidney. His face contorted with pain.

My attacker dragged me around a corner, out another door, and into the frigid December air. I swung backward with my foot, grazing the agent's calf. I still had my gun, so if I could get away, I might be able to land a good shot.

I tried another kick but slipped in the snow and lost my footing. The agent—a man, judging by the size of his biceps—grabbed my arm and slammed it against a tree, jarring my bones. Another blow.

Then another, and my gun fell to the ground as I lost all feeling in my fingers.

Still holding my arm, the agent brought it down toward his knee, but I twisted, leaned forward, and kicked back with my boot, hitting him in the groin. He shoved me to the ground. The black rubber grip on my gun handle stood out from the white of the snow. I scrambled for it, rolling to my back once it was in my hands. I pointed and shot, and the man went down just as a black boot kicked me. My gun went flying again.

Another agent stood to my right. Without my gun, I didn't stand a chance.

I staggered to my feet and ran. Fire burned from my throat down to my lungs. The land crested to a hill, and the river came into view. I barreled toward it, having no plan other than escape.

When I reached the bank, I cut left and quickened my steps, ignoring the voice in my head that said I couldn't run far enough, fast enough.

Someone crashed through the pines several feet downriver. It was the same agent who had kicked me.

He'd already outpaced me. I was dead.

I staggered back as he charged. I swung with a right-handed punch, but he dodged it easily and countered with an uppercut that landed at my side.

The force behind the blow threw me off-balance, and I stumbled off the riverbank and into the frigid water.

The agent jumped in after me and wrapped his hands into the folds of my jacket collar, yanking me to the surface.

He head-butted me, and I whipped back, the dull ache of the hit vibrating through my skull. My eyes blurred, crossed. My teeth chattered together. I couldn't think straight.

I blinked, trying to clear my vision, when I saw the man pull a needle from his inside jacket pocket. He bit off the orange cap and spit it out. The current rushed through my legs.

Summoning every ounce of strength I had left, I wrapped my hands around the agent's wrists and pushed upward, trying to kick his feet out from beneath him. But his stance was solid, and my legs felt weighted down. I couldn't get enough momentum to do any damage.

He brandished the needle with a closed fist, like a knife.

I fought against it, teeth gritted, feet planted in the river muck. But I was losing fast.

I tried to memorize the man's face, so that when I finally had the opportunity to get revenge, I would know exactly where to start.

A shadow stretched across us. Sam? Cas? Another agent?

The needle sank into my neck and I cried out.

The shadow came closer in a rush of movement. Whoever it was, he took the agent's head in his hands and yanked to the right. The man's neck popped and cracked, and he sank into the water, eyes wide and blank.

The current fought against me and I lost my footing.

"Come on," someone said, and grabbed a fold of my jacket, pulling me toward the bank with one quick yank. The needle was carefully extracted from my neck with gentle, gloved fingers.

When I was on solid ground again and I could focus, I looked up to see which of the boys had saved me, but it wasn't Sam or Nick or Cas.

It was Trev.

"What are you doing here?" I took a step back, getting a better look at his clothes. He was in full combat gear, too, the same gear all the other agents wore.

"Oh my God," I said.

He held up his hands. There was a rifle on his back, the strap slung across his chest. "I'm not going to hurt you."

Cas called my name somewhere in the distance.

"What are you doing here?" I repeated. Panic edged into my voice. "Did you set us up?"

"No, I didn't. I swear. I didn't know we were going to be here tonight. I just found out. And when I did...I came looking for you as soon as I could. I..." He paused, searching for the right words, in the way that only the old Trev would. The Trev I knew best. "Something else is going on here. I don't know what. But...be careful. Okay?"

"Anna!"

Cas again.

I didn't look away from Trev. I couldn't. He'd saved me. If he were here to set me up, I'd already be in the Branch's hands, wouldn't I?

I tried to think of all the other ways he could twist this to the Branch's advantage.

"You should go," Trev said. "Don't tell them I was here. Please."

When I didn't answer, he took a step closer. "Anna? Please?"

I let out a breath. "Fine."

He nodded, grabbing hold of the gun strap across his chest, as if he needed to lessen the weight on his back. "Be careful, please." He started off in the opposite direction.

"Thank you," I called quickly.

Trev looked over his shoulder. "You're welcome."

I watched as he disappeared into the woods.

"Anna, that you?" Cas said a second later.

"It's me."

"You okay?" He pushed aside a pine branch and came up beside me on the riverbank.

I was soaked. Shivering. Sore. "Yeah, I'm good."

"You gotta hurry up and get back to the lab, then."

Instantly I went into panic mode. Was something wrong with Sam or Nick? Had they been injured?

"Why?" I said quickly. "What happened?"

"We found your sister."

11

WHEN I RETURNED TO THE LAB, THE boys were pushing wounded agents into the last cell on the left.

"Lock it up," Sam ordered, and the handler punched in a series of commands on the control panel. The glass wall slid into place, sealing the remaining agents inside.

"Open the others," Sam said next, and the handler followed the order, freeing the two boys I'd seen when we'd first arrived.

I scanned the remaining cells. There was a third boy in the cell on the far right. He was tall, with short red hair, a face painted in freckles, and brown eyes that came across as more guarded than aggressive. When his cell opened, he cautiously walked out.

I looked at the cell next to his as a figure stepped out from the shadows.

It was a girl, a worried expression on her face, lips parted just enough to breathe a bubble of condensation on the glass. Bruises covered her left cheek. Her eye was swollen.

"Anna?" she said. Her lower lip trembled. "Is it really you?"

"Open that cell," Sam ordered.

"I am. Sorry," the handler said. "She just came in yesterday. I'm still getting used to the code to her room." The man punched in a series of numbers.

I hesitated in the center of the room, worried somehow that I was dreaming, that I was having a flashback.

"There, that's it," the handler said, and the cell opened and Dani burst out, tears streaming down her face. She lunged at me, frail arms wrapping around my neck. The faint scent of bar soap wafted from her.

Slowly, stupidly, I returned the hug and Dani trembled in my arms. "I can't believe it's you," she said. "I've been searching for so long."

She sobbed harder.

I didn't know how to comfort her.

Dani finally pulled away, put her hands on either side of my face. She was taller than me by a few inches, skinnier by at least ten pounds.

"Are you okay?" she asked. "Are you—" She looked over my shoulder at who I could only guess was Sam. Her eyes welled again and she stepped around me to wrap Sam in a hug with the same ferocity as the hug she'd given me.

"You found her. Thank you. Thank you for keeping her safe."

She pulled away and kissed him gently on the cheek. Sam immediately flicked his attention to me, checking my reaction.

I dodged his stare.

"We should get out of here," I said.

For once, Nick backed me up. "They'll send another team as soon as this one misses their check-in."

Cas started plucking things off the dead men and women. Mostly guns. Some clips.

"We taking these guys?" Nick asked, nodding at the three boys we'd released from their cells.

"For now," Sam answered. "At least long enough for them to adjust."

And for us to question them.

Cas appeared at my side. "Here," he said, handing me a black leather jacket. "Looks like you took a dip, huh?"

I frowned. "Not by choice." I took the offering and examined it. "Any bullet holes or blood?"

"Not that I could find."

The fact that I was stealing clothing off dead people was too ludicrous for me to process. I tried not to even think about it as I tore off my soaked jacket and slipped into the leather one. It was fleece-lined right down to the sleeve cuffs, and cropped at the waist. A thick, oversized hood hung down my back. The overwhelming scent of leather mixed with the sweet, crisp scent of perfume, and I wondered what kind of woman had worn this coat, had spritzed herself with perfume today not realizing that she'd lie dead in a basement by sunrise.

The red-haired boy stepped forward. "What about Thomas?"

It took us a second to realize he was referring to the handler. After opening Dani's cell, Thomas had made himself as small and inconspicuous as he could. He was pressed into the far corner, hands up.

"He nice to you?" Sam asked.

The boy shrugged. "I guess. He didn't hurt us, if that's what you're asking."

Sam gestured to Cas. "Put him in one of the cells."

Thomas, the handler, willingly entered the fourth cell. "Thank you for sparing me," he said as Sam hit the button to lock him inside.

"Don't thank us yet," Sam said. "Hard telling what Riley will do to you once he finds out you lost the *units*."

Thomas deflated as the realization settled in. Riley wasn't the forgiving type.

"Let's go," Sam said.

I looked over my shoulder at the woman whose coat I now wore. I'd come to terms with taking the life of anyone associated with the Branch. They knew what they were getting into when they signed up for the job. But that didn't mean I didn't feel remorse.

Before we escaped Branch headquarters, I'd killed the man in charge. Connor. Killing him at the time had been easy. It was what came after that tormented me the most.

I still saw his face in my head almost every day. I wondered how long I would see that woman's face, too.

Maybe forever.

I thought about saying a prayer, or some final words to send the woman's spirit off or whatever it was you were supposed to do to respect the dead. But all I could come up with was *Thanks for the jacket*, and I whispered it as I filed out the door.

12

I'D GOTTEN USED TO STAYING IN AN
actual house, so I wasn't exactly thrilled about having to rent a motel
room. The décor was garish. The sheets were stained. And the windows were painted shut. When I'd pointed this out to Sam, that we
had zero alternate exits, he'd grumbled something about it only being
temporary.

He split us between two rooms, with him, Dani, the red-haired
boy, and me in the first room. Cas, Nick, and the other two boys,
Jimmy and Matt, were in the second.

The red-haired boy, whose name was Greg, sat in the chair in the
corner. Dani sat on the edge of the bed, across from Sam and me.

"Tell us everything," Sam said.

Dani worried at her lower lip. "I thought you were dead. Both of you. For a very long time, that's what I believed." She inhaled, leveled her shoulders. "I've been in hiding ever since you were captured," she said to Sam. "I was shot, and the Branch left me in a field, probably assuming I'd bleed out. But I survived. And Anna…" She blinked, and several tears escaped her eyes. She swiped them away quickly with delicate finger. "I thought you were killed with our parents. And then I heard a couple of months ago, from one of my old contacts in the Branch, that you two had popped back up, that you'd escaped some top secret facility in New York.

"So I did some digging into a few old Branch contacts and got a couple of leads. I went looking for you, but Riley found me first. I think they were planning to use me as bait."

"Makes sense," Sam said.

She nodded and smiled. "Thankfully you found me before they could set their plan in motion."

I scooted closer to Sam. I desperately wanted to take his hand in mine, if only for the comfort, but I knew it wasn't the right time. If Dani didn't know about Sam and me being together, there was no telling how she'd take the news.

"So…what did they do to you?" Dani asked me. "While you were in that lab?"

That was a long story, and one I didn't feel like telling right now.

"Well, I just learned about you a few months ago," I said. "I didn't know I had a sister until then."

"They altered your memories." She shook her head, closed her eyes. "I'm so sorry." She scrubbed at her face, and when she dropped her hands, she was staring right at me. "So you really don't know me from a complete stranger, do you?"

I wasn't sure how much to tell. I had flashes every now and then, but I hadn't told Sam yet, and I didn't even know how reliable they were.

"Not really."

She pursed her lips, then said, "They'll come back eventually. I can help fill in whatever blanks you have, if you want."

"Thanks."

"You're next," Sam said, nodding at Greg, who'd been silent nearly the whole drive there. "You remember anything before that lab?"

Greg shook his head. "None of us do."

"How long have you been there?"

"Six months."

That wasn't very much time compared to how long we'd been in the farmhouse.

"Anything else? Anything that might be useful?"

Greg folded his hands across his midsection as he thought. He was extremely fit, but then, almost everyone associated with the Branch was.

"Nothing I can think of," he answered. "I wish I could help, man. I owe you big for getting us out." He sat forward, propping his elbows on his knees. "You're one of us, aren't you? The Branch gave you the Altered drug?"

Sam nodded. "Did they tell you why you were here?"

"They said we had to be quarantined because we'd reacted badly to the drug. Said we'd signed up for the program back before we lost our memories. Said that our heads were empty *because* of the treatments."

"You believe that now?" Sam asked.

"No. You're locked up long enough, you start asking questions. And when those questions go unanswered, you lose faith that you're being told the truth."

"The Branch doesn't know the meaning of the word," I said, and the bed squeaked as I shifted. "If you want my advice, don't believe anything the Branch has told you. It's all a lie."

I looked across the space between Dani and me. The Branch had told me she'd died, but if I knew Riley and Connor at all, I suspected they'd known for a while that she was alive.

Which meant they'd been waiting for the perfect opportunity to use her against Sam and me. Play her like a pawn.

But she was safe now.

The Branch had failed.

Nick met Sam and me outside while Cas stood watch over the other boys.

"So, what do you think?" Nick asked, shoving his hands in his coat pockets. "They a threat to us?"

Sam scanned the parking lot. There weren't a lot of people checked in to Nuva Boulevard Motel. Only one other vehicle was parked in the lot.

"If they've been genetically altered like us," Sam answered, "then yes, they pose a threat. But that depends on whose side they're on. So far it seems like they're grateful we helped them escape."

Nick snorted. "We didn't *help* them escape. We did all the goddamn work."

"You know what I mean, Nick."

I stepped between them. "We need to focus on where we go next. We can't cart the others around with us. It's too many people to deal with."

"Agreed," Nick said. The wind kicked up, and a curl of dark hair fell across his forehead.

"We can't just cut them loose," Sam argued. "They're trained assassins with no memories. And who knows what else the Branch was doing to them."

"You think they have a programmed commander?" I asked.

All of us went silent as we considered the possibilities.

"If Riley is the commander..." Nick said, and trailed off.

"Then having them around is a huge risk."

"What about Dani?" Nick said.

"What *about* her?" I asked.

"She was in the lab. Who knows what they could have done to her in that amount of time. Or maybe this was their plan all along. Maybe there's a tracking device on her."

"Then I'll check her," I said.

Sam sighed, the collar of his jacket shielding his face, catching his breath before it hit the frigid air. He turned to Nick. "Dani isn't up for discussion. We'll check all of them for tracking devices, and in the morning, we'll send the boys on their way."

"Fine," Nick said, though his tone of voice said it was anything but.

13

WHILE SAM, NICK, AND CAS CHECKED
the boys for tracking devices in the other motel room, I checked Dani.

I shut and locked the door. Dani stood fidgeting near the beds.
"So, where do we start?"

Here, in the bright fluorescent lights, her hair almost looked fire
red. Her eyes, a soft shade of green, were more vibrant.

She was real. My only sister.

But thinking it didn't make it feel truer. There was still a huge
disconnect between what I knew and what I felt. I knew I had a sister,
but that didn't mean I knew what it *felt* like to have one. I didn't
love her, not the way a little sister should, because I couldn't remember her.

"Let's start above the waist. Do you mind taking your shirt off?" I asked carefully.

She laughed. "No, I don't mind. You've seen me naked before."

She grasped her tank top at the hem and tugged it over her head. She was wearing a simple black racerback bra beneath. Her stomach was flat, the muscles clearly defined. Where there wasn't muscle, there were bones jutting out beneath the skin.

She tossed me her shirt. I ran my fingers along the hems, then worked over the fabric, looking for something that felt out of place. I found nothing.

Dani lifted the straps of her bra, checking the material. "Good here."

"Let's look for implants, then." I went to her side, and she turned around, baring her back. I started in her hair like Sam had instructed, feeling with two fingers for anything that shouldn't be there beneath the skin. I tried to work quickly, feeling the onset of nervousness. Sweat was beading on my forehead.

"Sam still looks the same," Dani said after I asked her to lift her arms.

"That's the alterations. They age at a slower rate than everyone else." I paused. "Your files said you were given the anti-aging drug, too. Did you know?"

"Yes. I meant...Sam hasn't changed as a person. He still keeps his hair short. Still more comfortable in jeans and a plain jacket than anything else. No badass agent-wear for him."

My throat tightened and my heart sped up as I thought about asking her all the things I'd wanted to ask someone when it came to Sam.

"Did he laugh back then?"

She shrugged as I ran my hands down her sides. "If you mean was he happy, no. Not really. Or if he was, he didn't show it often. Sam's always been very guarded."

After she checked her chest, we moved on to her pants. When we found nothing, I started at her toes.

"You and Sam are together, aren't you?"

I looked up at her. Sadness was pinched in the space between her eyebrows.

"What makes you say that?"

"Call it sister's intuition. Plus..." She glanced away, and her expression softened. "He orbits you."

I stood up. Dani had called Sam a boyfriend once. I didn't know where that left us.

"Do you still love him?" I asked.

"Yes."

My throat narrowed. "I didn't know... until it was too late, that you and he had been together."

"You don't have to apologize." She hung her head, and a lock of hair fell in front of her face. "I came to terms with losing him a long time ago." She looked up and smiled. "At least I know he's in good hands." She took a step toward me. "I have no intention of coming between you and Sam. I hope you know that."

I nodded. "Thank you."

She smiled. "Now, we should probably finish up before Sam freaks out." She laughed, and the sound stirred something old, something forgotten.

My vision teetered.

"Anna?" Dani ducked to look at me straight on. "You okay?"

I blinked but couldn't seem to focus on her. Everything on the edges was blurry, and everything in the center of my vision was smattered with flecks of white light.

"What's wrong? Do you want me to get Sam?"

"No," I said, but the word came out too breathy, too quiet.

Was it another flashback? Why here? Why now?

"I'm getting Sam," Dani said and started for the door.

I tried to stop her but stumbled, pitching forward.

The sound of paper scraping against paper.
The sound of a voice.
"How long are you here?"

The question echoed in my head. It was my voice asking it.

"Just tonight," Dani answered.

The flashback took hold of me, and the motel room faded away, the smell of cleaner and iron disappearing, replaced with the smell of pine and flowers and something smoky.

We were in a bedroom. Mine, I thought. From my old house. My old life.

I sat cross-legged on the bed, and Dani sat next to me.

I must have pouted, because she laughed and pushed the hair behind my ear. "Don't be sad, bird."

"I don't like it when you're gone. Dad is mean, and Mom doesn't say or do anything. I'm so bored."

Dani stiffened. "How is Dad mean?"

"I don't know. He yells a lot."

"Has he..." Her voice cracked. "Did he hit you again? I mean, when you get in trouble? Or when he yells?"

I frowned. I couldn't remember him hitting me ever, so I said, "No. I don't think so."

Dani relaxed and blew out a breath. She curled her index finger and thumb, cupping my chin. "I'll come back for you. I swear it. You just have to be patient."

"I don't want to be patient."

"It won't be much longer now. Sam's gonna help me get you out. It'll be an adventure."

I brightened. "Will Nick go with us?"

Dani rolled her eyes. "Why would you ever want that crabby pants to come with us?"

"I don't know." I picked at the blanket spread out beneath us. "He's nice to me. He showed me how to make these." I held up a piece of paper that was folded into a bird. "He said his mom showed him how."

Dani held the bird by its sharp, pointed tail. "Did he, now? Well, in that case, maybe we should bring him along. Maybe he can fold us a boat out of paper and we can sail across the ocean."

I rolled my eyes. "That's dumb. It would sink."

She laughed again and smoothed down my hair. "You never know. Anything is possible, bird, if you wish for it hard enough."

───────────────

My head thunked against something solid. I opened my eyes, saw Sam peering down at me. It was his knee I'd hit. My head was cradled in his lap. "Hey," he said.

"What happened?" I asked groggily.

"You passed out." He looked across the room. I sat up just enough to see Dani and the others. Suspicion creased the lines around Sam's mouth.

I shook my head, silently telling him that Dani hadn't hurt me.

Cas sat next to me on the bed and put his hand on my leg. "I offered to give you mouth-to-mouth, but Sam vetoed. I don't know why. I said I wouldn't use tongue."

I snickered. Sam frowned and pried Cas's hand away by the fingers. "I'm sure she appreciates your concern," he said, "but she was breathing just fine."

Cas shrugged. "Minor detail."

I eyed the new boys, wondering if they saw me as weak now. I would hate it if they did. But the two assigned to Cas and Nick's room weren't even looking at me. They were perusing a magazine that had a race car on the cover with a barely clothed woman on the hood.

Greg was telling Dani something about his sudden craving for hamburgers.

If they thought me weak or deserving of pity, they weren't showing it. At least not yet.

"You need anything?" Sam asked.

"I don't know." I rubbed at my temple. "I have a pounding headache. Maybe some—"

Nick tossed me an individual packet of painkillers. Cas brought over a glass of water.

"Thanks, you guys," I said to both of them before ripping into the packaging. I downed both pills with one gulp of water. These things were becoming diet staples. How many painkillers could one person consume before they keeled over?

"So, did the boys check out?" I asked Sam.

"Everything looked good. No trackers, as far as we could tell."

"You prepping them on what to do when we part ways?"

He nodded. "I'm taking Greg to the store to buy some basics."

"Good." I sat up, and my vision swam again. I suddenly felt like I might puke. That had been the worst flashback yet.

"So, what happened?" Sam asked, edging closer. His arm wound around my waist, his fingers hesitating at the exposed flesh of my hitched-up shirt. He checked to see if Dani was paying attention, and I realized he didn't know yet that she was aware of our relationship.

"She knows," I whispered. "About us."

He looked down at me again. "You told her?"

"She already knew."

He pursed his lips, nodded, and looked away. Sometimes it was easy to read Sam, and other times, like now, it was like there was a brick wall between us. Did he feel guilty? Had he wanted to tell Dani himself?

When he turned back to me, he asked again, "What happened?" and I realized the conversation about Dani was over.

"I don't know."

He narrowed his eyes, as if he suspected I was withholding something important. "You don't remember anything?"

I wanted to share the flashback with him, but not now when we had an audience. Later, maybe, if we managed to get a free minute.

"I just got dizzy, is all."

"Uh-huh." He leaned in and kissed the top of my head. "Get some rest while I'm gone. And that's not a suggestion."

"Yes, sir."

He gave me a look that said he was not amused with my humor. To Greg he said, "You ready? We should get going."

Greg pushed away from the wall where he'd been chatting with Dani.

"We'll be back in an hour," Sam said. "No one leaves this room. Got it?"

We all murmured our assent as they left.

14

MOONLIGHT POURED THROUGH THE PARTED
curtains and pooled on the dingy gray carpet. I couldn't sleep.
Instead, I was counting the cracks in the ceiling as Sam breathed
softly next to me. In the other bed, Dani faced away, toward the
bathroom. Greg was sleeping on the floor. He'd insisted.

My body was a maze of sore spots. It was hard to find a comfortable position.

Sam shifted next to me. "What's wrong?" he whispered.

"Nothing."

"You're lying." He said it as a fact, not an accusation.

I sighed and rubbed my eyes. "Earlier... it wasn't that I got dizzy.
I had a flashback. A pretty intense one."

He sat up, leaning on an elbow. "Why didn't you tell me?"

"You were busy and I—"

"Anna." He stopped me. "You have to be honest about this shit, or—"

"Like *you're* honest?" I kept my voice low, worried about waking the others. "You never tell me anything. You haven't said a word about how you feel about Dani being back. And I know you have to *feel* something. You loved her once."

He hung his head. "Her being here changes nothing."

"You can't predict the future. You have no way of knowing what memories might return or how they'll make you feel. This could change everything."

"It won't." He leaned in, his fingers threaded through my hair. He kissed me gently. Then more eagerly, a second time.

I slid closer and moved to tug his shirt off when he stopped me. That's when I noticed the peppering of bruises all over his torso.

He was in worse shape than I was.

"I didn't know your injuries were so bad."

He sighed. "I've been shot, remember? A few bruises are nothing."

"Except you were trying to keep it from me," I pointed out.

"Because I knew you'd worry."

We locked eyes in the semidarkness. A smiled edged onto my lips. "Yes. You're probably right. I would worry. But that's because I love you. I get to worry."

He reached over and pushed a lock of hair away from my face, fingers trailing along my temple. I closed my eyes. I liked it when he touched me. It didn't even have to be intimate. It was like my nerve endings weren't truly functioning until they were beneath Sam's fingers.

"I love you, too," he said. "Now try to get some sleep. If you're having flashbacks, you'll need it."

We curled up together, my back pressed against his chest, his arm around my waist. I slid my fingers into his and squeezed.

I fell asleep quickly.

The next morning, just after sunrise, we stood in a loose circle in the middle of a park. Everything was covered with a fresh layer of snow and glittered in the early sunlight.

The new boys had their packs slung over their shoulders. Sam had also bought them each a winter jacket.

"Thanks for this, man," Greg said to Sam, and shook his hand. "We got any way of calling you in the future? In case something comes back? Or if we need your help?"

Sam nodded. "I programmed a number into your prepaids."

"Thanks," they murmured.

"And thanks again for busting us out," Greg added.

Cas shifted his weight from one foot to the other. "I'm going to miss you guys."

"You hardly know them," I said.

"I know them enough to know I'll miss them." He went over and gave each boy a half hug, half handshake before saluting them. "Till we meet again, gentlemen."

The boys laughed and saluted him in return.

Dani went over and hugged each one, too. "I didn't know you all very long, but I can tell you're the good guys. Be vigilant, all right?"

Greg grinned. "We w—" His expression changed instantly. The grin disappeared from his face. He dropped his pack on the ground. Matt and Jimmy did, too.

"Greg?" Dani said. "Something—"

He punched her. A powerful shot to the cheek. She flew backward.

"What the hell?" Cas shouted as Jimmy charged straight for him.

"Shit," Nick said just before Greg threw a punch in his direction. Nick ducked, and Sam stepped in, landing a solid blow to Greg's chest. He staggered back, gasping for air.

I hurried to Dani's side. "Are you okay?" I rolled her over, and she spat blood in the snow.

"What is happening?" she said.

I looked up. The boys were in an all-out brawl with the others. And it didn't look good.

Greg had Cas pinned facedown in the snow until Nick kicked Greg in the back. Matt and Sam were circling each other. Jimmy leapt onto Nick's back and wound him tight in a headlock.

"We should go," Dani said in a rush. She grabbed my hand and pulled me in the opposite direction. "Before it gets worse. Sam would want you safe until it's over, right?"

I shook my head. "I'm not leaving them."

"Anna!" Dani pulled harder. "They'll kill us."

"No, they won't. I won't let them. Stay here." I started into the fray.

Jimmy swung Cas around, slamming him into a tree. Cas grunted, eyes squeezed shut for a fraction of a second. Just long enough for Jimmy to punch Cas in the side. Cas's knees buckled. Jimmy grabbed a hunk of his hair and dragged him up.

I had a clear shot at Jimmy's back.

I ran at him. But less than a foot away, he dropped Cas and swung at me with a backhanded punch. I ducked. He kicked me in the shin. I staggered away, the dull throb of the hit vibrating clear up to my thigh.

He threw another punch that I managed to deflect, then another that caught me across the top of the head. I tried to ignore the throbbing in my skull as he wound back for another blow, exposing his right side. I thrust upward with a jab, landing it in his ribs.

He paused through the pain, giving me the opening I needed.

I kicked him once in the knee, then again in the kidney.

He dropped to one knee, and I punched him in the temple, knocking him unconscious.

I turned to the others. Sam had Matt on the ground on his stomach. He took Matt's head in his hands and slammed it to the ground. Blood poured from Matt's nose, and he stopped moving.

Sam stood up. Cas sidled in next to me. Nick wiped blood from his face as Greg stared at him.

"The only one remaining," Nick said to Greg. "You think you can take all of us?"

Greg didn't answer. His eyes were blank as he looked us over, like he was calculating the odds in his head.

He turned around and ran.

Nick started after him, but Sam called out, "Let him go."

Nick scowled. "He just attacked us! And we almost lost."

Sam watched Greg disappear around a street corner. "I don't think he knew what he was doing. You see the looks on their faces? Like nobody was home." He ran the sleeve of his jacket over his mouth, wiping away the blood. "Something wasn't right."

Dani staggered to her feet. "It was like they were brainwashed." She winced and gently fingered her now doubly swollen jaw.

"Anyone see them on a cell phone before this?" Sam asked. We all shook our heads.

"We should get out of here," Nick said, "in case there are agents in the area."

"What about them?" Cas asked, nudging Jimmy with the toe of his boot.

Sam looked around the park. There were no witnesses. No cameras. "Leave them here."

"Poor bastards," Cas added before slinging an arm around my shoulders. "Help me to the car, Banana? I need some assistance."

I snorted. "I'm sure you do."

Together, we hobbled away but kept our eyes on the surrounding area just in case. If the Branch could control people remotely now, there was no telling what else they were capable of.

15

SAM HOPPED A CHAIN-LINK FENCE IN
the backyard of an empty house that was for sale.

We needed a place to clean up, to regroup. I could only imagine
the conversation we were about to have. Nick scowled and fidgeted
next to me, and I could tell he was dying to say I told you so. So I
figured I might as well get it over with.

"Go ahead," I said.

"What?" he asked.

"You think Trev set us up."

He leaned against the fence as Sam slunk to the rear door and
worked on the lock. "You're damn right I think he set us up. He gave
us that location. We broke those guys out of that lab. We walked

right into their plan. They gave us ticking time bombs, and we practically stuffed them in our back pocket."

I looked over at Dani, who was trying to pretend like she wasn't listening. "We found my sister, though," I said. "That's what we went there for."

"Yeah, they used her as bait. And you bit into it."

He was right, of course. I had. Maybe they'd set the whole thing up, right down to kidnapping Dani in that alley behind the grocery store. Riley had been second-in-command on the Altered program. He knew us well.

But I didn't think Trev had known about the plan.

He'd been there that night, yes, but he'd saved me.

If their goal was to take us out, Trev could have let that agent drug me in the river and I'd already be locked up in some Branch cell.

I would have told Nick if Trev hadn't asked me to keep it quiet.

And why had he?

The back door to the empty house swung open, and Sam waved us inside.

The place was freezing. We entered into a long, narrow kitchen. There was a room beyond that and another in front. All of the bedrooms were apparently upstairs.

Cas found a leftover towel in the upstairs hall closet. Thankfully, the water was still running. Unfortunately, it wasn't hot water. We cleaned up as best we could with what we had.

"So," Cas said as we hung around the kitchen, "we got a plan?"

I helped Dani wipe the blood from her face. She winced when I hit a sore spot, and I muttered a quick apology.

"I have an idea," Nick said. "We go to Branch headquarters and blow that goddamn place apart."

I couldn't help but smile at that. Nick was usually the voice of reason. No unnecessary risk—self-preservation, always.

Clearly he was pissed. And I couldn't blame him. How long could we run from the Branch? They obviously weren't keen on letting us fade into the distance. We knew too much. We were too valuable.

We couldn't ever be free as long as the Branch was out there. They would keep making supersoldiers, altering them until they were faster, stronger, smarter than us. We'd just walked into one of their traps. What would they do next?

"We can't go after them without a plan," Sam said. He scrubbed at his face with the palms of his hands. "It would help if we knew more about what happened with Greg and the others.

"If they went through the same Altered program that we did, then their commander could have ordered them to kill us."

"But they had no contact with anyone," I pointed out. "And they have to follow a direct order immediately after receiving it. There isn't a delayed response on that."

Sam nodded. "What are the other explanations?"

"Brainwashed," Nick said.

"I was thinking the same thing."

Sam paced for a minute. "But what set them off?"

Nick leaned into the counter and crossed his arms over his chest. "Something, or someone, in the area could have set them off with a laser or maybe a flash of light. It could be anything. It could have been something one of us said unknowingly."

Sam stopped pacing. "Greg said they'd been in that lab for six months." His gaze grew distant as he thought. "Cas and I were at Branch headquarters a little over two months ago. Which means, if they'd already perfected this new kind of programming with Greg and his team..."

Silence.

We all knew what he was insinuating. If the technology was complete and they had the means and the opportunity, why not brainwash Sam and Cas, too, as insurance?

"But..." I started, trying to come up with a viable excuse to talk him down. "Like you said, Greg and his team were in the lab six months. The Branch had you and Cas for only twenty-four hours."

"That's plenty of time to implant something. Some new programming. Some new alteration. Whatever it is they've created."

Dani nodded. "It's true, Anna. It takes only a few hours for a drug to take hold."

I rounded on her. "How would you know?"

She shrank away, and immediately I regretted snapping at her.

"I'm sorry. It's just... we don't have any of the facts."

"That's true," Sam said. "And until we do, none of us are safe."

"We'll be careful—" I said, but he cut me off.

"We should separate."

"No."

"Anna," Sam said.

"No." My heart fluttered in my chest. "You were at the Branch two months ago. If they programmed you, why wouldn't they have activated you by now?"

"Maybe they're just waiting for an opening."

"And maybe they want us to separate. Did you consider that? Divide the pack. We're weaker apart."

Sam rocked his shoulders back, clearly irritated with me. "Did you not see what happened at that park?" He pointed out the window, even though the park was miles and miles away now. "One minute they were fine, the next minute they were blank-faced and attacking. That could have been me. Me attacking you. I can't risk that."

"I'm not letting you leave."

"You don't have a choice." He gestured at Nick. "You stay with Anna. Cas and Dani are coming with me. As far as we know, she's been brainwashed, too."

I glanced at Nick. "Nick doesn't want to be saddled with me. He's not a babysitter."

Nick didn't say anything.

"He'll be nice," Cas said. "Right, Nicky?"

"Don't fucking call me Nicky."

"See?" I said, pointing at Nick. I was being petty and whiny, but I didn't care. I didn't want us to separate. I didn't want to be left alone with Nick while Dani went with Sam.

Sam started for the front of the house. "It's for the best, Anna," he said over a shoulder. "I'll find an extra vehicle for you two so you have transportation, and then we're splitting up. I don't want any more arguments about it."

The door slammed shut a second later.

⸻

Nick took watch at the front of the house. Cas stayed at the back door. I went to the dining room and sat on the white carpet, leaning against the wall. I drew my knees up and stared out the sliding glass door that led to a weather-worn deck.

Dani sat next to me.

Now, alone with her, I didn't know what to say or do. What had we been like before all this? I wondered if we'd talked for hours on end. If she'd given me advice about boys and homework, and if she'd done my hair and made me breakfast.

I wondered a lot of things about her.

"So," she said.

"So."

"I know it seems like a bad idea, separating, but Sam's only doing it for your safety. He's always been protective." There was a note of sadness in her voice.

I turned to her. "I'm sorry."

"About what?"

"I don't know. Everything." I rested my chin against my knees. "I wish we would have met again under different circumstances."

She sighed. "Me, too."

"When I found out the Branch had taken my memories, that I had a different life before the farmhouse, I knew I had to fill in the missing pieces. But there isn't much left, is there?" I glanced over at her. "You're the only part that remains."

"Not true. We still have Uncle Will."

I sat up straighter. "Uncle Will? You've seen him?"

Dani nodded, and a wispy strand of hair fell from her ponytail. "He's the one who learned you and Sam had escaped the lab. He's got great contacts within the Branch. Actually, I think you might know one of them. Sura? She used to be married to your handler at the farmhouse."

The mention of Sura brought on a new wave of sorrow. My dad had led me to believe Sura was my mother and that she was dead. And when I found out the latter was untrue, I'd been ecstatic. I'd met her, only to learn she'd never had any children, that my dad had lied about her being my mother, too.

And then she'd been shot right in front of me.

In my head, I could still hear the *pop* of the bullet.

I squeezed my eyes shut.

"Anna, did you hear me?" Dani said.

"What? Sorry. No."

"I said I could put you in touch with Uncle Will. He'd like that. He might have information, too. He's always digging into the Branch's movements. He used to be friends with the person who founded it. Now he does whatever he can to sabotage their missions."

I raised a brow. "Really?"

She smiled. "Pretty badass, our family, huh?"

"I guess so."

I recalled something Trev said to me the morning he helped us escape Branch headquarters, that the Branch wouldn't stop looking for us. I'd wondered at the time who "they" were with Connor dead.

"How big is the Branch?" I asked Dani. "Who's coming after us this time? Do you know?"

Dani reached over and squeezed my hand. "One question at a time, bird."

Our eyes met, the old nickname hanging in the air between us. It was an immediate reminder of what we'd lost, and it made something stir. A connection to her, a spark of our past, the wick of my old life catching fire.

"You remember," she said softly. "I used to call you 'bird' all the time. Because you ate—"

"Like one," I finished. I didn't know how I knew that, but the answer was there, on the tip of my tongue and spilling out over my lips.

"Yeah." Her green eyes lit up. "I could only ever get you to eat peanut butter and jelly sandwiches. I had to cut the crusts off."

"In all of my flashbacks, you were always the one taking care of me. Why? Where were our parents?"

She stiffened. "Our parents weren't the best kind of parents."

"What do you mean?"

"I mean...they were busy."

"Did they work a lot?"

She nodded. "Something like that."

"Did you mind taking care of me?"

"No. Never." She smiled. "I liked it, even."

"I'm sorry," I said again, looking down at my feet.

"You keep saying that." She nudged me with her shoulder.

"It's just...I wish I could remember more."

Because I can see how happy it makes you, I thought. A large part of my life, or at least the one I could remember, had been spent trying to make others—the boys and my dad—happy. And some habits died harder than others. I wanted to make the smile reappear on Dani's face. But I didn't know how to force myself to feel something for her or to remember all of the things we'd shared.

"None of this is your fault." Her voice shook. "I was the one who failed you. I was the one who lost you that night. I was the one who couldn't get to you all those years you were missing."

"That night?" I repeated.

"What?"

I turned sideways. "You said you were the one who lost me that night. The night our parents died? You were there? Did you see what happened?"

"No," she said with a quick shake of her head. "I meant I lost you that night because I *wasn't* there."

"Oh." I deflated, the hope escaping me as quickly as it'd come. I hadn't realized until that very second how badly I wanted to know the details of how our parents died.

"Uncle Will knows what happened that night," Dani said. "He might tell you if you asked."

"Really?"

She nodded. "If I can get a message to him that you want to meet up, would you go?"

"Of course."

"He'll be in Port Cadia."

My shoulders sank an inch. Port Cadia was my hometown, but it was also the place where the Branch had captured Sam twice now. Once before the farmhouse, and again two months ago when we went back to retrieve the files Sam had hidden there.

Sam would kill me if he knew I went to Port Cadia. But... if he wasn't with me...

Nick might agree to go if I gave him a good enough reason.

The front door opened.

"Everything go all right?" I heard Nick ask Sam.

Sam muttered a response.

"Get Uncle Will the message," I whispered to Dani.

She nodded with a grin.

I'd reach Port Cadia one way or the other. With or without Nick.

16

I SAID MY GOOD-BYES TO CAS AND
Dani before Sam walked Nick and me over to our new stolen vehicle.
It was a nondescript car painted the color of wet charcoal. The windows were lightly tinted. That always made me feel a bit safer when traveling by car.

As Nick loaded a supplies bag in the trunk, Sam led me around the car to the passenger side. "Let me see your gun," he said.

I handed it over.

The street was deserted this time of day, and I wondered if everyone who lived in this neighborhood was off doing normal stuff like working in offices and having coffee with friends. What I wouldn't give to have a normal life.

Sam dropped out the clip from my gun and made sure it was fully loaded before sliding it back in place.

"When will you come back?" I asked.

He opened my jacket and returned my gun to my shoulder holster. "I don't know. I'll call your dad and see if he knows of any other programs. We'll go from there. Until then, call only if you have to. I don't want to risk one of us saying the wrong thing."

Snow started to fall in small, lazy flakes that clung to Sam's shoulders. I brushed them clean. "And what am I supposed to do? I have to help."

He shook his head. "Take a break. Rest."

We fell into silence. There was one more thing that needed to be discussed, but neither of us was brave enough to bring it up first.

Dani.

"Stop giving me that look," Sam said with a tilt of his head.

"What look?"

"Like you're worried I'm going to hook up with your sister."

"That's a very specific look."

He put an arm around my shoulders and dragged me closer. "You don't have to worry. I don't know how many times I have to tell you that."

"I'm not."

"You are."

I picked at the cuff of my jacket. "Do you still have flashbacks from before? About her?"

He didn't say anything for the longest time, then, "Yes."

"What are they about?"

He sighed. "Nothing important."

"You're lying."

"You don't want to know."

"Sam."

His fingers threaded with mine. His were long, solid, and they made mine look tiny in comparison. The veins in his hand stood, pronounced, running through his knuckles. Out of all the perfect parts of him, his hands were what I loved most.

And I realized with sudden, crashing despair that I hadn't ever sketched his hands.

The images I had seared into my brain weren't reliable. What I needed was something more tangible. Pictures. Sketches. Words on the page.

And I'd failed at recording Sam.

Don't go, I thought. I wanted to shout it at him, beg him not to leave. But he would never listen.

He leaned into me, his other hand cupping the side of my face. He kissed me softly, slowly, in a way that was more than just lips on lips. A kiss that was not only physical but something more, something deeper. A kiss I felt in my soul.

A kiss that felt like a good-bye.

A kiss I didn't want to end.

I always wanted more of Sam. Always.

When he pulled away, I kept my eyes closed a second longer, memorizing the feel of him, the smell of him, wanting nothing else to distract me before I burned the memory to a place that I hoped would outlive even the Branch's tampering.

"Be careful," I said.

"You, too."

And then he was gone.

17

NICK DROVE OUT OF TOWN AND TOOK
the freeway. I couldn't tell where he was headed. Maybe he didn't
know, either.

I leaned my forehead against the window and closed my eyes as I
felt a familiar burn deep in my sinuses. I didn't want to cry. Not now.
Not in front of Nick.

"It's not like they're dead," he said.

No, but it felt like I'd never see them again.

"I hope you don't keep doing that," he added. "Because we're not
going to get anything accomplished with you crying."

"And we're not going to get anything accomplished if you keep
acting like an asshole."

He went rigid. I tensed, knowing that I'd crossed a line.

But a hint of a smile spread over his face. "Now that we got the petty shit out of the way, why don't we make a plan? Unless you want to write in your diary about how sad you are and how you got saddled with the fucking asshole."

"It's not a diary," I muttered.

"Good. Because diaries are for douche bags."

I laughed. "Was that an indirect compliment?"

He furrowed his brow. "No."

"I'm pretty sure that was a compliment."

"I'm pretty sure you're irritating me."

"I wouldn't have it any other way."

"Great, so are we going to argue, or are we going to do something about this?"

"Do something about it," I said, and he nodded. "I have to go to Port Cadia."

"What?" he shouted.

"My uncle lives there. He might know something. He has contacts in the Branch."

"In case you forgot, the last time we went looking for one of your family members, we ended up screwed."

"Come on, Nick! What else are we going to do? Go to Branch headquarters and blow the place up?"

"Yes."

I sighed. "Please. This is important to me. And I think meeting him could help. He might know something worthwhile."

And he was there the night my parents died, I thought. I would have used it as additional ammo if I were talking to anyone other than Nick. But he didn't want to learn about his past. He'd made that painfully clear. So he wouldn't understand my need to learn about mine.

"Nick?" I tried again.

"Do you know exactly where to find him?"

"Dani is going to contact him."

He grumbled in the back of his throat. "This keeps getting better and better."

"Please."

"Fine. But if Sam finds out about this..."

"He won't."

"Oh, yes, he will. It's Sam we're talking about."

"Just head to Port Cadia, and I'll deal with Sam when the time comes."

What would he do when he found out where we were headed? I didn't think I wanted to know.

Nick took several back roads as we headed north. He found a local rock station, and the music filled the silence between us.

I dug in my bag for my journal, finding it wedged on the bottom beneath a hairbrush and an extra gun clip. I grabbed my set of colored pencils next. It was always hard to predict how long we'd be on the road and whether or not there'd be a free minute to sketch.

I could go from eating a turkey sandwich to getting shot at in the span of two seconds. Drawing seemed like the last thing I should be wasting my time with. But it helped anchor me to the real world. It was something that was familiar, something normal.

So I started sketching.

I didn't have a particular image in my head, and I was fresh out of travel magazines for inspiration. I considered asking Nick to stop at a grocery store so I could buy something to browse, but then I reminded myself this was Nick I was talking about, and no way would he stop for a magazine run.

As usual, I started with a warm-up. I had a few pages in the very back that I'd designated as my doodle pages. There were waves and hearts and 3-D cubes. I scribbled in a goldfish, then an umbrella, then more hearts.

I looked over at Nick. His left hand rested at the top of the steering wheel. His right hand held tightly to the stick shift between us. His black hair curled around his ears and over the collar of his coat. Even in profile, with only a sliver of his eyes in view, I was taken aback by how shockingly blue they were. How he had this way of looking at things like he didn't care at all, when I knew deep down he was taking everything in. Every detail. He forgot nothing. And he would use it against you as soon as the perfect opportunity presented itself.

Nick downshifted when he got stuck behind a semi waiting for the car in the next lane to pass. His jaw tensed. His eyebrows sank in frustration.

I turned to a fresh page and started drawing. I thought I'd sketch Nick driving, but the further I got into the sketch, the more I realized it wasn't of Nick sitting next to me, now. It was of him pushing someone into a darkened room, panic creased around his eyes. There was a four-poster bed behind him.

I was studying the image, trying to figure out if it was real or imagined, when the journal was snatched from my hands.

I looked up. The car was parked in front of a gas pump. Nick spread the journal open on the steering wheel.

"You drew this just now?" he asked.

"Yes."

"Did I tell you about this?"

I frowned. "No."

He stared at the penciled image for a long time. A car pulled up at the pump on the other side of us.

"What is it, Nick?" I finally asked.

"This is one of my flashbacks."

I sat forward. "It is? What is it about? Who are you pushing?"

He slammed the journal shut and tossed it back to me. He climbed out of the car and went around to the gas tank. I climbed out, too. The frigid air hit me before I was ready for it. Salt crunched beneath my boots.

"Nick? Who is it?" I asked again, even though I had a sudden sinking feeling that I knew exactly who it was.

Nick flipped open the gas tank, unscrewed the cap. He punched at the buttons on the gas pump, and it beeped in response.

I took a step closer. "It was me, wasn't it?"

"Yes. Okay. It was you."

My breath puffed out between us. "What happened? Why were you shoving me in a room—"

"It was a closet. And I don't know."

I pressed my back against the side of the car. Sam and I had been to my old house. In one of the rooms, we'd found the empty frame of an old four-poster bed. In the closet, I'd found a picture of me and Dani, stuffed in a keepsake box along with a—

I gasped. "A paper crane."

Nick furrowed his brow. "What?"

"In the closet in the house in Port Cadia, I'd found a box with a picture of me and Dani and a flattened paper crane." A million theories started running through my head. I paced. "And in one of my flashbacks, there was a boy sitting on my bed with me. Dani and Sam were fighting down the hall. I could hear them and I was upset, so the boy showed me how to make a paper crane to distract me." I met his eyes, suddenly realizing what my brain had been trying to tell me for a while now. "That boy was you."

His eyes grew distant. "My mother showed me how," he said in a voice barely above a whisper.

I nodded. "That's what you told me in the flashback."

"It's the only thing about her I remember. I don't even know what she looked like." He blinked and pulled the gas pump from the car. "What kind of person leaves their kid, anyway? A godda—"

He cut himself off and looked away.

Just like that, our moment was over. Nick was back to being Nick, but I was going to celebrate the victory, no matter how minuscule it was. Nick had opened up. Maybe there was a part of him that did care after all.

———

Dani called later that morning. "I got a message out to Uncle Will that I found you and that I was sending you his way. Hopefully I'll hear from him later with a specific meeting time and place."

"Thanks. Does Sam know you're doing this?"

"No. I called while he and Cas were in the bathroom. We're at a rest stop right now."

I exhaled. "Thanks for that. I don't want him knowing yet."

Nick snickered beside me.

"No problem," Dani said. "Will you make it to Port Cadia by tonight?"

"Yeah, I think so. We're getting food right now and then we'll be back on the road."

"Good. I'll call as soon as I know more."

We said our good-byes, and I tossed the prepaid into the center console.

"What do you want to eat?" Nick asked.

"I don't know. I'm not picky."

He whipped the car into the nearest shopping lot and parked in front of a little café in the lower level of a huge redbrick office building.

Wind chimes rang out above us as we opened the door. The barista perked up. "What can I get for you guys?" she asked, readjusting the visor of her green hat. Her ponytail was wound in a loose bun and hung out the back.

"I just want black coffee," Nick said.

"Nothing to eat?" I asked.

"Nope." He sauntered off and picked a table near the windows but not directly in front of them.

I ordered a coffee and a sandwich and waited for our order to come up. When it did, I shuffled over to the bar area so I could add tons of cream and sugar to my cup.

My stomach grumbled at the sight of the food and the smell of the fresh-brewed coffee. I tore open a sugar packet and upended it over the cup. Out the corner of my eye, I saw Nick shove his chair back and wind his way through the occupied tables.

"Here's your coffee," I said to him.

"We have to go."

Instantly I was on alert. "Why?"

"Why do you think?"

I glanced out the front windows. A black Suburban was parked in the street. And there were agents headed for the café.

"Oh my God."

Nick gave me a shove toward the back of the building. We turned left down a hallway. There was an alternate exit there next to the stairwell and an elevator. Nick peered out the tiny window in the exit door.

He cursed beneath his breath. "We have to go up."

"What?"

"Up the stairwell. Go."

The sound of wind chimes clanging together at the front door got me moving. In the stairwell, we rushed up an entire flight. I was extremely grateful for having the endurance to keep up with Nick.

"This way," Nick said and motioned me to the second floor. We entered a carpeted hallway. Two women in pencil skirts and suit jackets walked past. "Excuse me," Nick said. "Is there another exit in this building?"

The woman closest to him nodded and gestured with a tip of her head in the opposite direction. "On the east side of the building."

Nick smiled. "Thanks."

When the women walked away, Nick pushed me down the hall. We took several wrong turns, passing office after office before locating the second stairwell. Nick reached for the door at the same time it rushed open.

A gun was shoved in Nick's face. "Don't move," the agent said.

Nick put his hands up. A second agent came out of the stairwell. A woman. She positioned her gun on me.

Using his free hand, the man pressed a finger to his ear, to the device attached there.

"We got them," he said right before Nick pulled out his gun and shot him in the head.

18

THE FEMALE AGENT WIDENED HER EYES
and swung toward Nick. I ripped a fire extinguisher off the wall and
whacked her over the head with it. She dropped next to her fallen
partner.

"Jesus!" I shouted at Nick. "She had a gun on me. She could have
killed me!"

"Start stripping them."

"What?"

"Just do it."

I peeled off the woman's boots, then her pants. I tore off her hat,
and a cascade of brown hair fanned over the floor. I had to wrestle
with her jacket and T-shirt.

"Now what?" I asked.

Nick scanned the empty hallway before darting inside a darkened office. The door said it was an accounting business. "In here," he said. He dumped the first agent's clothes in a closet, but saved the walkie-talkie. I dumped the woman's clothes next to the other pile and shut the door.

"Out," Nick said, pointing at the window.

Without questioning this time, I unlatched the window and shoved upward. The wind pulsed inside, rattling the bamboo blinds. I eased onto the ledge, which overlooked an adjoining office building. Nick came out next and shut the window quietly. He held the agent's earpiece between us. I could hear voices faintly through the device.

"Unit one, check in," someone said.

"Unit one, roger," a woman said.

"Unit two, check in."

Silence.

"Unit two, check in."

Nick spoke through a tiny microphone on the device's cord. "Unit two momentarily knocked unconscious. We seem to be... um...missing our clothes."

More silence. My teeth began chattering together as I pressed against the building's exterior. I could already feel my nose turning red in the cold.

"All units," the person said, "identify your partners. Suspects are believed to be posing as agents in uniform. I repeat, identify your partners."

A smirk touched the corners of Nick's lips. "Ready to jump?" he asked.

The next building was also a two-story building, but it was at least six feet shorter.

"What if I break my leg?" I said, more to myself than to Nick.

"What if an agent hits you with a tranq and takes you into headquarters, and they wipe your memory?"

I cringed. "Point taken."

"On three," he said. "One. Two. Three."

I jumped and my arms spun. When I hit the roof of the next building, I tucked into a forward roll to avoid breaking any bones. Nick did the same, and we took off at a run. We leapt over a small ledge between buildings.

A bullet hit the brick chimney two feet to my left. I slid over a patch of ice as I slowed, glancing over my shoulder.

Riley was standing in the window we'd just escaped from, his gun aimed right at me.

Nick yanked me in the opposite direction. Another bullet blazed overhead, pinging off a return air vent.

Nick ran to the edge of the roof, where the row of buildings ended in an alley. He didn't slow, and every instinct told me to pull back, dig my feet in before I leapt to my death. But Nick had never put me in harm's way.

I had to trust him. The alternative wasn't any safer.

We leapt off the roof. My stomach dropped to my knees. The air in my lungs fluttered in the back of my throat. I didn't even have the presence of mind to scream.

We landed in a Dumpster piled high with black garbage bags, enough to soften our landing. Without pausing, I jumped out onto solid ground, with Nick just behind me.

"Go right," he said, so I did.

At the mouth of the alley, Nick and I slid to a stop as an agent rounded the corner, his gun directed at us.

"Got 'em," the agent said. "Alley between West Fifty-Fifth and Huntley." To us he said, "Don't move."

But, as I knew all too well, Nick didn't like orders, and I was beginning to feel the same way.

I grabbed the agent's gun, stepped to the left, shoved up. A shot went off, the bullet lodging itself in the wall next to us. Nick swept in, kicking the man in his now exposed left side. A rib cracked. Nick kicked again. The man's grip loosened on his gun, and I wrenched it from his hands as his legs buckled. Nick kneed him in the jaw. I shot him in the leg.

Nick and I looked at each other. Something unspoken passed between us. An understanding, maybe. That if we stopped butting heads so much and started working together, we'd be unstoppable.

"Go," Nick said. Our path was clear for now, but who knew how long we had before more agents arrived.

I could guarantee it wasn't long enough.

19

WE RAN FOR FIVE MILES. STRAIGHT.

To say that I felt like dying at the end would be an understatement. Nick didn't even seem winded. Since our car was all the way in the other direction and stealing another car would take time out in the open that we didn't have, we hid in a nondescript diner, waiting for things to cool off.

Nick held his coffee between both hands as he watched the door and the front windows warily.

On our five-mile jog, Nick had worn the agent's earpiece so he could track the Branch's movements. When they'd located their downed agent at West Fifty-Fifth Street, they'd followed our footprints in the snow to Lucgrove Avenue, where we'd essentially disappeared into a brick wall.

That was thanks to Nick, who devised a plan to use empty milk crates to climb onto the roof of a sandwich shop. He'd knocked the crates over as he hung from the roof's ledge to cover what we'd done. The Branch was probably savvy enough to figure it out, but we weren't leaving any clues if we could help it.

From there, we covered the span of an entire block by rooftop, the city spread out around us. Hastings wasn't a large metropolitan area, but I could make out a few skyscrapers in the distance and the streets below us were busy with foot traffic despite the January weather. When Nick and I finally climbed down a fire escape, our footsteps were easily lost in the hundreds already pressed into the snow.

That was forty-five minutes ago, and Nick hadn't spoken since we'd ordered our coffee.

When his phone rang in his pocket, he nearly lurched out of his chair.

"You okay?" I asked.

He checked the phone's display, ignoring the question. "It's for you."

The screen read Sam's number. "Hey," I said when I answered, trying to act casual when I was anything but.

"Where are you?" Sam said, his tone not at all conversational. If anything, it was suspicious.

I looked at Nick. He raised a brow.

"In a diner."

"In Michigan?"

I winced. How did he figure these things out so quickly?

"I traced the phone," he answered, sensing my unspoken question. "You're two hundred miles north of where you're supposed to be. Did Nick talk you into something?"

"No." If anything, it was me who talked *him* into coming.

"Where are you going, Anna?"

I sighed. "I want to dig into my family's past. I want to know more." That was a close truth.

"Don't tell me you're going to Port Cadia."

"Okay. I won't."

"Anna."

"What else am I doing right now, Sam?"

He let out a breath. "Please don't go to Port Cadia without me."

I closed my eyes. I was so tired. I was tired of arguing. Tired of being treated like I was somehow more fragile than the boys. I might be a girl, but that didn't mean I needed to be coddled. I contemplated confessing that we'd encountered agents, that we'd seen Riley, that we'd had to fight for our lives and won. But he was already annoyed, and telling him all that would only make it worse.

"We're already halfway there," I answered. "I'm not turning back."

If Uncle Will could give us anything, anything at all, it was worth meeting him. Plus I wanted to see him in person. See one more member of my forgotten family.

"Goddamn it." There was a long pause before he spoke again. "Be safe. Stay alert like I taught you."

"I will."

Nick reached across the table and snatched the phone from my ear. To Sam, he said, "Have you had any flashbacks about that night five years ago?"

I guessed Sam needed no clarification for what night Nick was referring to—the night my parents died, the night Sam and the others had supposedly been caught by the Branch.

Nick scanned the diner while he listened to whatever Sam's response was. "If you remember anything, call me." A pause. "Because something isn't right about it, but I don't know what yet." Another pause. A grumble. "I will."

He tapped the phone off with a finger and went back to analyzing every single person who entered the diner.

"What made you question Sam about that night?" I said gently.

"If I knew, I wouldn't have had to ask the question."

I slumped in the chair, stretching my legs out. He was so difficult sometimes.

I didn't expect him to elaborate, not after that comment. But maybe there was something in the coffee that loosened him up, because he added, "I don't trust your sister."

I frowned. "Why?"

"I don't know. The fact that she's been gone five years, that we found her in the same lab as those brainwashed kids. Or how about the fact that she seems perfectly okay with you and Sam being together? Like she already knew."

"How was she supposed to take it? Bitterly? For one, she has been gone for five years. She moved on. And two, I'm her sister."

He screwed up his face. "So because you share blood, stealing her boyfriend is okay?"

I cocked my head to the side. "I did not steal Sam."

The front door opened, and Nick's attention flicked to it briefly before settling back on me. "Call it whatever you want. But if you ask me, she came to terms with it a little too quickly."

I shook my head. "She's my sister. I trust her."

"You don't even know her."

"We're family."

Nick tightened his hold on his coffee cup. "Family means nothing. Your own blood can do fucked-up things to you."

I stared at him. Did he know about his dad? That he used to abuse Nick?

I reached across the table. "Nick, I—"

He shrank away. "Are you ready to get out of here?"

I pulled my hand back.

He tossed a twenty on the table and walked toward the door, shoulders hunched.

Months ago, Nick had told me he thought it was better for him if he didn't remember his past. His exact words were "I might not remember who I was before all this, but I can bet it wasn't all sunshine and fucking roses."

I still sometimes wondered if that was true, if knowing would somehow make everything worse. Eventually Nick would have to talk about his past, wouldn't he? It seemed like out of all of us, not talking about his issues or memories would damage him the most. Maybe that's why he'd ended up with the Branch in the first place, because he hadn't worked through the things his dad had done to him. But for me, it was different. There was a voice in the back of my head that said I would never feel complete if I didn't fill in the missing pieces.

I wanted to know about my family, my past, who I was and why I was here, what had sent me on this path.

I only hoped Uncle Will could help.

20

OLD-FASHIONED LAMPPOSTS ON THE SIDE-
walk had flicked on since we'd been inside the diner and
now illuminated the street in a golden glow. The temperature had
dropped, too, if that was even possible. It just went from cold to
colder.

We walked a mile or so before Nick stole another car, thank
God. As soon as the engine was warm enough, I blasted the heat.
Feeling returned to my toes and fingers. I curled up against the
passenger-side door and closed my eyes, feeling the heaviness of sleep
creeping in.

White light flashed behind my lids.

I saw Dani through a crack in a doorway.

"We had a deal," she said.

"And I stuck to that deal," a man answered.

"He's relapsed, though. He's not better, and Anna isn't safe here."

"What do you want me to do? Would you like me to take her in? Start her out young?"

Dani scowled. "No. I don't want her having any part of this."

"Then quit asking me to make exceptions."

"I'm not. I'm just asking you to care for once."

"Oh, Dani," he said with an edge of laughter. "I care. That's exactly why we're here now, having this conversation. I care too goddamn much."

A phone rang somewhere in the distance.

I jolted awake.

"It's for you," Nick said, handing me the prepaid.

I blinked the sleep out of my eyes and took the phone, reading the screen before I answered. It was Sam's number again.

"Hello?"

"Hey." But it wasn't Sam. It was Dani. "I got a meeting set up with Uncle Will."

I straightened in the bucket seat. "You did. Where?"

"There's a bar in Port Cadia. Molly's, it's called. He'll be there tonight. Eight PM"

"All right. Thank you for doing this."

"No problem." She paused. "Is Nick being nice to you?"

"As nice as he can be."

Dani laughed. "That's all you can ask for."

"So..." I turned to the window, away from Nick, as if that would afford any privacy. "How's Sam? Is he... okay?"

"Sam is fine," Dani said. "You don't have to worry."

"And Cas?"

"Cas is Cas."

She paused, then, "I should go. Be careful, bird."

After promising her I would, we hung up.

"So?" Nick said.

"My uncle should be at a bar tonight."

"So what do we do before then?"

I shrugged. "I don't know. But I wouldn't mind taking a nap in a proper bed."

Nick veered to the right, to the next freeway exit. "How about breakfast, and then we find somewhere to crash?"

I nodded. "Yes, please. I could go for a gigantic pile of pancakes right about now."

"With brown sugar," Nick said in a voice so low I barely heard him.

"What?"

His jaw tensed. "Just... try it with brown sugar. And syrup. And butter."

"All right," I said, slightly suspicious.

It was the best combination of sweet and buttery I'd ever tasted. I covered the stack of pancakes with butter, drizzled it with pure maple syrup, and then sprinkled brown sugar on top.

It was like heaven.

"Have you had it this way?" I asked Nick once I'd sopped up the last of the syrup. He shook his head. "Then how did you know I'd like it?"

He emptied his cup of coffee. "I just did."

I tilted my head to the side. "Come on."

Our waitress, an older woman with a long braid of gray-brown hair, swooped in, clearing our plates. "Room for dessert?" she asked.

I was stuffed. Maybe more stuffed than I needed to be. Sam had told me overeating was one of the biggest mistakes we could make. We could never know when Riley or the Branch would swoop in, and having a full stomach made you lethargic and slow. "Only eat for fuel," he'd said. And I'd definitely just eaten for pleasure.

"No, thank you," I answered. Nick shook his head.

"I'll have your bill ready for you in just a minute." She hurried off.

I turned back to Nick. "So?"

He shrugged again. "I just knew, all right?"

I narrowed my eyes. "You remembered, didn't you? I used to like brown sugar on my pancakes when I was a kid?" Nick just stared at me, which was answer enough. "How do you know all these things about me?"

Another shrug. He avoided looking at me.

I smiled. "Maybe you didn't hate me so much back then."

He snorted. "Doubtful."

I ticked off the things I knew about our past. In a flashback, he was with me while Dani and Sam fought. He'd shown me how to make a paper crane. He knew how I liked my pancakes. And in my drawing, the one where he was pushing me inside the closet, I had to wonder if he wasn't pushing me inside to be mean, but instead to hide me from something.

And if so, what?

Or who?

───────

After we ate, we drove around for another hour. We didn't have much money left, not enough to rent a room somewhere, and it was far too cold to nap in the vehicle. Besides, the heat had started malfunctioning, so it hovered between blowing out cold air and blowing out air that smelled like a basement.

Nick drove to a nicer part of town, where quaint cottages were stuck between mammoth houses, and all of them surrounded a lake. The road narrowed the farther north we went.

"Where are we going?" I asked.

"We're looking for a place to crash, remember?"

I sat forward, the seat belt tightening across me. "In someone else's house? What if they come home while we're there?"

"Shh. Just wait a damn second."

I grumbled but sat back.

Finally he slowed and pointed at a one-story gray brick cottage. "Look, the driveway hasn't been shoveled. There aren't any tracks in the snow, in the driveway, or on the front path up to the door." He nodded at the houses farther up the street. "See the icicles hanging off the roof?"

"Yeah."

"It means the heat's running. Now look at this place. See any icicles?"

I scanned the roof's edge. "No, not really."

"Means the heat is turned down so they can conserve it to keep the utilities low. It's probably a summer place."

"So no one will find us."

Nick nodded. "Exactly."

He pulled in the driveway and up on the side of the garage, partially hiding the car beneath a canopy of thick pines. We walked around to the back of the cottage. There was a small porch there, and a back door with an old aluminum screen on the outside. I held it open while Nick worked at the lock on the inner door.

I bounced on my feet, trying to ward off the numbness spreading through my toes. The temps were colder here, and the wind coming in off the lake was nearly icy. *Hurry up, Nick*, I thought.

The lock clicked open, and Nick pushed the door in. I barged past him into a mudroom. Water shoes and sandals were lined up on a black mat. Raincoats hung from hooks on the wall. Beach toys were stacked in crates in the corner. I relaxed. This was definitely a summer home.

I followed Nick through a small galley kitchen to the living room. There was a sectional couch covered in white sheets. Nick tugged them off with one pull. Dust swirled in the air.

"It's nice being out of the wind," I said, rubbing my arms, "but it's still freezing in here." I could see my breath.

"We'll only be here a few hours. I'll turn the heat up."

He located the thermostat in the makeshift dining room tucked in the back of the living room. "Seventy okay?" he asked and I nodded. He turned the dial, and the furnace ticked on a few seconds later. "Give it ten minutes, and it should warm up."

"Thank you. Really."

He looked at me, his expression hovering between his default scowl and something softer, more sympathetic. He didn't say anything in reply, so to combat the sudden, awkward silence, I started searching for a linen closet or a blanket hutch, for something to keep me warm while the house heated up.

I found an old fleece blanket in a bag under one of the beds. After giving it a good shake, I wrapped it around my shoulders and plopped onto the couch.

Better already.

It took all of one minute for my eyes to grow heavy and my head to droop.

"You can take a nap," Nick said. "I'll keep watch."

"You don't mind?"

He shook his head. "That's what we're here for anyway."

"What about you?"

He pulled a chair up to the front window and parted the curtains just enough to see out. "I'll be fine."

"Are you sure? Because I could take the first—"

"Anna." He silenced me with a look. "Go to sleep."

"All right," I said, because I was exhausted. I lay down, curling onto my side, the blanket tucked around me.

It didn't take long for me to pass out.

21

WHEN I WOKE UP, AN OLD MEMORY HOVERED
in the sleepy haze, like a word I'd forgotten, just out of my reach. I
knew the feeling of it, the shape of it, but not any of the finer details,
the details that mattered.

Whatever the memory was, I knew instantly that it'd been important, and I sat up cursing.

Nick looked at me with a frown. He was hunched in the chair,
still positioned at the front window. There was a beer in his hand, the
top popped open. His hair was even more disheveled since I last saw
him. I wondered absently if he'd moved at all, or if he'd been in that
spot the whole time I slept. He must have moved to at least find a beer
ferreted away somewhere in this place.

He looked beyond exhausted.

I set my feet to the floor and rubbed my eyes. "I had another flashback, I think."

"You know who was there?"

The way he asked the question made me wonder if he was asking because he wanted to know if *he* was there. Since he'd been in a lot of my memories, I thought it was a good chance the answer was yes.

"I'm not sure," I said, because that was the easiest response. "But there was..."

Blood. I paused, and looked down at my hands. A phantom sensation, warmth spreading between my fingers. Here in the present, my hands were pale, dry, cracked along one knuckle from the cold. Not covered in blood, but the sensation was overwhelming. I could almost feel it beneath my fingernails, feel it running down my arms.

I shook the image away.

Maybe I was going crazy.

"What?" Nick prompted.

"Nothing." I stood. "Any idea where the bathroom is?"

He nodded down the hall. "Second door on the right."

"Does the water work?"

"Yep."

Inside, I shut and locked the door and used the toilet. After washing my hands and face, I looked in the mirror.

My head was pounding. My eyes hurt deep into the sockets. When would I ever live a normal life? Like, go to bed not worrying about being ambushed in the middle of the night. And wake up looking refreshed, a whole day spread out before me. A day of possibilities.

I sighed and turned on the faucet to splash some warm water on my face when my vision cut out. Sight came back to me in flashes, like a dozen blinks in rapid succession.

I slammed my eyes shut, pressed the heels of my hands to my temples.

A scream. In my head.

What the hell was happening?

I was running. Through a hallway. People were shouting behind me. I slid into the bathroom, tore off the toilet tank lid, and plunged my hand into the freezing-cold water. I came up with a plastic zipper bag. There was a gun inside.

My knees buckled. I pitched to the side, scrambled for something to hold on to, but took a basket of toiletries down with me. Aluminum and glass containers clanged and shattered on the floor.

Blood on my hands. Running down my arm. Blood beneath my fingernails.

Something splintered and slammed against the wall. Hands shook me.

"Get Anna out of here," Dani said.

"Anna!" Nick shouted. "Can you hear me?"

Opening my eyes hurt and the light from the ceiling blinded me. The leftover haze of the flashback mixed with the present, and I wasn't sure what was real and what wasn't.

Nick crouched beside me, his fingers digging into my skull as he examined me. "What the hell happened?"

"Another flashback."

He looked over his shoulder at the shredded bathroom door. "New rule: Leave the door unlocked next time."

With his help, I climbed to my feet. My head swam a second but dissipated enough that I could pretend I was fine.

But was I?

When we'd first left the lab at the farmhouse, Sam had gone through several debilitating flashbacks once his system withdrew from the memory suppressants. My dad had told me once that Sam had gone through too many memory wipes and that's why his came back so violently.

As far as I knew, I'd had my memory wiped only once, right before I'd been placed at the farmhouse.

So why was I experiencing the same thing Sam had?

We hung around the summer cottage for several more hours while Nick tried to repair the bathroom door. He managed to get it back on its hinges, but there was no way to hide the caved middle where Nick had rammed a shoulder into it.

Just after seven PM, Nick turned down the heat and locked up the house. He walked with me to the passenger side of the car, as if he was afraid I might have another sudden flashback.

After I got in, I watched him as he rounded the front bumper, his face shrouded in darkness. I wasn't sure who this Nick was, the one who looked after me and helped me into the car and took a second to make sure I was all right.

Maybe this was more of the real Nick, a combination of the old him and the present-day him, who was a genetically altered badass.

Whoever he was, I liked him. And I hoped he stuck around.

It took us another half hour of driving before we reached Molly's bar. The clock in the dash said it was 7:45 when we parked in the lot.

Molly's was a two-story building on the edge of town. Music pumped through the thin redwood walls, and people were huddled together outside smoking cigarettes. An orange neon sign hung in the front window promising cold beer on tap.

"Let me lead," Nick said after he'd parked. "You think you'll recognize your uncle when you see him?"

"Yeah. There were pictures of him in the files."

"When you spot him, tell me before we approach. Got it?"

"Yes."

We climbed out, and I tightened my coat as we hurried across the parking lot.

As soon as Nick pulled open the front door, the smell of sweat and stale beer wafted out past us. Music thumped through the floor. The place was packed.

Nick guided me to a round table in the corner, where we were partially hidden by a support column.

I scanned the crowd. There was a big group of people in the opposite corner from us. A large man in denim overalls held on to an unlit cigarette as if the nicotine could be consumed through osmosis. A petite dark-haired girl guffawed at something her friend said.

Farther back, a couple made out in a booth. A cluster of girls slung back shots. An old man drained the last of his beer. And a lean, red-haired man—

"That's him," I whispered, leaning closer to Nick. "Back of the room. One o'clock."

I tried to act inconspicuous, but this man—Uncle Will—was the only living family member I had who might remember the details from the night I'd been taken by the Branch.

He looked similar to the man in the picture from my files. Red hair, cut short; freckles peppering his nose; wide-set eyes; and full lips, like Dani. I could see a lot of her in him, and it made me wonder what our dad looked like and what part of the family genes I'd inherited. I didn't have the red hair. I didn't have the same plump lips. I did have the freckles, but that seemed like the only thing I'd been given from the O'Brien side. Was I more like my mother? Did she have blond hair and hazel eyes and a nose that seemed too small for her face?

There was a man sitting next to Will, a beer in his hand. There was no drink in front of my uncle. He smiled at something his friend said.

I stood up.

Nick took my hand. "Wait."

"I've been waiting to meet my real family ever since I found out about them." I yanked my hand back. "I'm not waiting another minute longer."

The music changed from a quick rock song to bluegrass, and the crowd livened up as the room filled with the sharp twang of a banjo.

I crossed the room. My hands grew slick with sweat. I wasn't sure what my expectations were, but I knew more than anything that I wanted Uncle Will to like me.

He laughed again. His friend patted him on the back. Will looked up and spotted me. He paused.

Did he recognize me? Did I look like my real mother or father?

Will stood. His friend asked him something, but he didn't answer.

I stopped three feet from the table, hands hanging loosely by my sides. Now that I was here, I didn't know what to say or where to start.

"Anna," he said with a smile. "It's good to see you."

"Uncle Will?"

He nodded and came out from behind the table, wrapping his arms around me, squeezing tightly.

When he pulled back, he said to his friend, "Nathan, I'll call you later. I gotta go."

"Sure thing, buddy." Nathan grabbed his beer and sauntered off.

Hands still on my shoulders, Will stared at me for the longest time, as if he couldn't believe I was real. Nick edged closer.

Finally Will said, "We need to talk. Somewhere quieter, perhaps?" He looked over my shoulder at Nick. "He a friend of yours?"

I could feel Nick hovering just a foot or so away. I was both thankful and annoyed. "Yeah. A good friend."

"All right. Well, he can come, too. Follow me." Will set a hand between my shoulder blades and guided me out the front door. He gestured to a small pickup truck parked in the back of the lot. "That's my car. Did you want to ride with me or..." He trailed off, eyeing Nick.

"We'll follow you," Nick answered.

"All right. My place is over on Washington. We can talk there." He fidgeted with his keys and they clattered together. "So I guess I'll see you in a few minutes."

I nodded. "Sure."

In our car, Nick turned to me. "I don't like this."

I rolled my eyes. "You don't like anything. Or anyone."

"Yeah, well, I especially don't like this."

"I'm not backing out now. Will could know something. And even if he doesn't, he's my uncle. I want to at least talk to him." My voice cracked, and I inhaled deeply. "Please, Nick?"

He turned on the engine and followed Will out of the parking lot. "If we get shot at tonight, I'm blaming you."

Uncle Will lived in a second-floor apartment across from the public library. Sam often told me that if it seemed safe, it probably wasn't, and there was nothing more innocent than a public library. So while every part of me said to relax, I kept my guard up, just in case.

The apartment was small, with one bedroom in the back, and a kitchenette connected to the living space. There was a couch in the living room, worn on the left side, as if Uncle Will spent most of his time in that one spot watching the old TV propped up on a rickety table.

There were dishes in the strainer but none in the sink. The small two-seater table was bare and freshly polished. It smelled like Pine-Sol in here. And cigar smoke.

"Have a seat," Will said.

I took the right side of the couch, and Nick sat on the arm next to me. I didn't have to look at him to know he was tense, ready to go off on a moment's notice.

Will pulled up a chair from the table in the kitchen. "I don't even know what to say." He laughed, but it turned into a drawn-out sigh. "You look so grown-up." He rubbed his hands together. "So, tell me, what did you want to talk about?"

"A few things, I guess. First, Dani said you had contacts in the Branch?"

"I do."

I threaded my hands together and tucked them into my lap.

"Well, two nights ago, we found Dani in a Branch lab, along with three other boys."

"Others like Sam?" Will asked, his tone guarded.

"Yes, but...something was different." I explained what had happened to Greg when we'd tried saying our good-byes.

Will digested the information and crossed one leg over the other knee. "Interesting. I've heard talk about the Branch looking into new programming. You think they were somehow activated?"

"Yes. But we're not sure how."

"Could be a code word."

Nick cracked a knuckle. "What are the chances that one of us would have said the right word at the right time?"

Will shrugged. "If it was a common word..."

"Do you think there's a way to reverse it?" I asked.

"Sure. There usually is, but I wouldn't know how. Or even where to begin."

I sighed. I was afraid of that.

"One other thing," I said.

"Sure. Anything."

"Dani said you were there the night my parents died."

Will bowed his head, the fan of his lashes meeting the freckles on his cheeks as he squeezed his eyes shut. "I was," he said quietly.

I sensed Nick watching me.

"What happened that night?"

Will looked up. Back rigid. Hands tightened into fists. "Sam happened. He killed your parents. Took you away."

All the air in my lungs rushed out in one long gasp.

"That can't be right," I said.

Will uncrossed his legs. "I was there, Anna. I saw it happen."

My stomach seesawed.

Sam killed my parents?

"But...why?" I breathed.

Will lifted a shoulder. "It was my understanding that your parents were trying to keep Dani from him. They knew he'd gotten himself into some trouble with the Branch and if he took Dani with him, there was a good chance she'd be killed, too. I showed up just minutes before Sam pulled a gun. I tried to stop him, but he was too strong." Tears welled in Will's eyes as he looked up at me. "I'm so sorry I couldn't stop him."

I had the sudden urge to puke.

Sam had killed my parents.

And he was with Dani right now.

Another thought occurred to me. "Were the others there? Nick or Cas?"

Will glanced at Nick. "No."

Relief, though minuscule and not at all comforting, flooded through me. "And what about me? Where was I?"

"You were hiding in your room."

"You have any proof that Sam did it?" Nick asked.

Will spread out his hands. "Nothing on me. I had heard from one of my old contacts that the events of that night were detailed in Sam's Branch files. I haven't seen them, though."

Trev had given us all the files and information he could find about us back when we escaped from Branch headquarters. I had only skimmed through Sam's files. It was possible I hadn't found the appropriate one yet.

Had Sam read that file and not told us? Did he remember?

The piece of paper I'd found in his bedside table, right before we left the cabin. The note with all of the names written in Sam's handwriting.

My parents had been on that list.

Was it possible he was documenting the names of the people he'd killed as he remembered them?

If that was true, he'd known about my parents for a while now.

I leapt to my feet. "I have to go."

Nick stood behind me. Will stood, too. "Anna. Wait," Will said. "Please don't rush out of here like this. I've only just found you again. Stay here. You and Nick both. You can have a home-cooked meal and a good night's sleep."

"We're not staying here," Nick said.

Will took a step toward me. "At least tell me where you're going. Or give me your number. I don't want to lose you a second time." Tears again, clouding his eyes. "You and Dani are all I have left of my brother."

Nick slipped between Will and me. "Give us your number, and *we'll* call you."

Will pursed his lips but nodded. He tore off a piece of the newspaper sitting on the end table and scribbled down a number on the margin. "That's my cell. I'll be sure to keep it on."

I folded the paper and slid it into my pocket. "Thank you."

He nodded and walked us to the door. "Be careful around Sam," he said as I stepped through the doorway. "I don't know if you're in touch with him or what. But he's dangerous and reckless and stronger than any normal man should be."

I knew that. I knew how strong Sam was. It was one of the things I loved about him.

But now, instead of it being an asset, it was something to fear.

22

AS SOON AS WE WERE ON THE ROAD

again, I told Nick about the list I'd found in Sam's bedside table.

"You have it on you?" Nick asked.

I did. I'd folded it into a tiny square and tucked it into a pair of socks in my bag. I retrieved it, and Nick pulled off the road to read.

"Has he said anything to you about this?" I asked.

Nick shook his head.

"So what do you think?"

"I don't know," he said. "Look at this. He was organizing them into groups. The asterisks are confirmed missions. I recognize a few of the names. Joseph Badgley, for one. We were on that mission together."

"It's a kill sheet, isn't it?"

He didn't hesitate. "Yes."

"So the question marks…"

"Mean he's not sure if he killed them or not."

My parents' names had question marks next to them. But the simple fact that they were on the list was enough. He had remembered something about that night, something to make him question his role in their deaths, and he hadn't told me.

"I just wish I could remember," I muttered. "That'd solve everything."

"Yeah, but shit's never that easy."

I sank into the bucket seat as Nick pulled onto the road, headed in the opposite direction. "Where are we going?"

"I'm taking you to Sam."

I straightened. "What? You know where they are?"

Nick nodded. "Sam's been keeping me in the loop."

I blew out a breath. "So it's okay for you to know where they are but not me? What, he doesn't trust me?"

Nick scowled. "It was to protect you."

I grumbled to myself. "How long before we get there?"

"About three hours."

"Great," I said, but I knew three hours wasn't enough time to prepare myself. What was I going to say to Sam once I saw him? How did I even broach the subject?

I didn't want it to be true. Hating Sam seemed worse than losing him. And I couldn't stand the thought of either.

Nick took us to Grand Rapids, where Sam, Cas, and Dani were apparently squatting in a condominium complex that was in foreclosure.

The condo they had picked out was so palatial, my anger instantly doubled.

Nick and I had been on the road for nearly twenty-four hours straight, and we'd broken into a cottage that was coated in dust and smelled like a musty basement. And here Sam was in a penthouse condo with three bedrooms, two bathrooms, granite countertops, and indoor pool access. The pool was probably not in working order, but still.

What made everything worse was that Dani looked even more gorgeous than when I'd last seen her. Like she'd morphed into a goddess overnight. She wore a pair of skinny jeans and a sweater that hugged her tiny waist. Her hair was clean and shiny, while mine was greasy and snarled. There was still blood on my clothes and dirt beneath my fingernails.

And the whole situation just felt wrong.

They all stared at me, and the room grew quiet and awkward.

Nick stood shoulder to shoulder with me, and ironically, his presence made me more confident, bolder, and I didn't hold anything back.

"Having fun, are you?" I said. "If I'd known you guys were taking a vacation, I would have stuffed myself in one of your suitcases."

Sam sighed. "Is that really necessary?"

I stalked across the open space to where he stood at the kitchen island and slapped the list down on the countertop. "I found this in our room at the cabin."

He looked at the piece of paper with a blank expression. "What is it?"

"You tell me."

He grabbed the list and my hand and steered me down the hallway. Nick came with us, maybe because he wanted to hear the explanation with his own ears. Or maybe because he was afraid of what might happen between me and Sam if Sam admitted the truth, whatever it was.

We grouped in an empty bedroom and Sam closed the door behind us.

"Did you kill my parents?" I blurted.

"Anna—" he started.

"Did you?"

His shoulders sank. "I don't know."

"Have you had flashbacks to that night?"

"Yes."

"And what do you see?"

A vein in his forehead rose beneath the skin. "You, mostly."

"What am I doing?"

"Crying."

"Is there blood on my hands?"

"Yes."

I inhaled through my nose as I saw a flash of twelve-year-old me looking down at my mother, blood covering the front of her. Was the blood on my hands hers? Was the memory real?

"Did you see who killed them?" I asked again.

Sam didn't look away as he said, "No. I haven't been able to remember that part yet."

"It's supposedly in your files," Nick said.

Sam shook his head. "I've read my files over and over again. There's no mention of that night."

"Where's the flash drive and the laptop?"

"Wait here," he said and disappeared to the front of the condo. He came back a second later and handed them over. "If you find something, let me know." I grabbed for the laptop, but he held on tight. "Please?"

"I will."

"We'll move to another condo in the meantime," he said. "Just to be safe."

The way he looked at me, like he was more lost than I was, made me soften. I wanted to reach out to him. I wanted to touch him. I wanted none of this to be true. "I'll call you if I find something," I said, right before he walked out the door.

23

WITH THE OTHERS GONE, I GOT COM-
fortable in the smaller bedroom with a view that overlooked the
street. I propped myself in a corner, laptop in my lap, and started
reading.

I skimmed through all the files I'd already read. There were a lot
of medical files and logs like the ones we'd used at the farmhouse lab.
Seeing them with Sam's name scrawled across the top stirred old
memories.

I used to love doing the logs at home. So much so that I'd gone
down there to do the dailies on my last birthday because there was
nowhere else I'd have rather been.

Of course, the boys had other ideas. They'd planned me a surprise party, which was an incredible feat, considering they weren't

allowed out of their cells. They'd put it together with my dad, picking which decorations to get, what kind of food to have. They'd even put in personal requests for my gifts.

It was the first time I could remember anyone doing anything special for me.

When I got down there, the lights were off. My dad had gone ahead of me an hour before, so I knew it was odd. "Dad?" I'd called.

The lights flickered on. "Surprise!" they yelled, though Nick's was more of a disgruntled murmur.

Green streamers had been taped to the front of the boys' cells. There were balloons everywhere, even inside the boys' rooms. A cake sat on a folding table in the center of the lab and read in scrolling pink gel, HAPPY BIRTHDAY, ANNA.

At first I was speechless, afraid that if I said anything, I'd burst into tears.

When I finally had control of myself, I asked, "Whose idea was this?"

Sam, at the front of his room, a thin sheet of Plexiglas between us, answered, "It was a mutual decision," while Cas and Trev shook their heads.

"It was Sam's idea," Cas said, grinning, and Sam shifted his gaze to the floor, hiding his eyes.

I went to his room first. My stomach filled with butterflies. "It was?"

He looked up, his expression warmer, brighter than I'd ever seen it. "You do a lot for us. It was the least we could do."

Later, after cake and ice cream, after my dad went upstairs complaining of exhaustion, the boys gave me their gifts.

Cas got me a paranormal romance novel. "They're making it into a movie," he said. "So it must be good, right?" I didn't have the heart to tell him I'd already read it and its sequel.

Trev got me a new set of colored pencils, ones he knew I'd been coveting. Nick got me a scarf and muttered something about being careful not to choke myself with it.

At Sam's request, I'd gone to his room last. He put something in the hatch, and I opened it on my side. It wasn't wrapped, but then, gift-wrapping didn't seem like his kind of thing anyway. I felt the texture of the hardcover first, and when I pulled it out, I realized it was a blank journal.

He hadn't known about my mother's journal yet, or at least not the details. I'd brought it down to the lab every now and then to sketch, or scribble notes, but there was no way he could have known how important it was to me.

"Someday," he said, "you'll run out of pages in your notebook, and I wanted to be sure you had something new to start with."

It was a simple book. The cover was black cloth with no writing on it. I opened it up to smooth, hand-pressed pages that were creamy and thick between my fingers.

I was about to flip it shut when I caught sight of writing on the front page.

To Anna, it read.

Because you are happiest when you are sketching.

—Sam

It was the first time I saw myself through someone else's eyes. The first time I realized Sam watched me when I wasn't paying attention and regarded me as someone other than just my dad's lab assistant.

It was the first time I felt truly justified in liking him, or even loving him, the way I did.

And if I'd been thinking about it when we left the farmhouse, I would have grabbed Sam's gift along with my mother's journal. I'd regretted leaving it behind.

How could *that* Sam, the one who I'd fallen in love with in the lab, be the same person who'd killed my parents?

I didn't want to believe it. I came up with excuse after excuse to explain it away.

Maybe he was confused. Maybe it was self-defense.

Or maybe Uncle Will was wrong.

I continued through the files. There were pages and pages of transcripts from Sam's initial tests. His IQ test scores. His physical exams. There was even a log of his sleeping patterns.

I kept going, digging deeper and deeper, checking the files I'd ignored in the beginning because of their nondescript titles. Names like TEMPLATES and MAINTENANCE. Finally, something caught my eye: a file marked O'BRIEN in the REFERENCE folder. I clicked through and found another file called O'BRIEN INCIDENT.

How had I missed this before?

I opened the document. There were dates, times of debriefing. A lot of pieces were missing because whoever had written the document hadn't actually been at the house that night.

But there was a "reliable eyewitness," so I scrolled until I found the witness's info.

He or she hadn't been named, but there was a transcript of the meeting with a Branch agent.

> Witness: Sam made everyone go into the foyer. He had a gun. Mr. and Mrs. O'Brien tried shielding their daughter, but Sam dragged her away, toward the front door.
> "No one move," Sam had said.
> Mr. and Mrs. O'Brien held up their hands. Sam pointed the gun at them.
> Agent: What was Dani doing at this point?
> Witness: Crying. She kept asking Sam to put the gun down.

I paused. Dani had said she wasn't there that night. Was she lying? Or maybe she didn't remember? Had the Branch stolen that memory from her, too?

I kept reading.

> When Sam wasn't looking, Mr. O'Brien made a grab for the gun. When Sam realized what was happening, he shot.

Mr. O'Brien went down. Mrs. O'Brien started screaming, so Sam shot her, too.

Agent: And then what?

Witness: Dani attacked him. She was yelling at him and hitting him. That's when the Branch agents showed up and Dani ran out the back door.

I set down the laptop, as the urge to vomit rose in my throat. Sam *had* killed my parents. He was the whole reason we were here now, why we'd been in the program at the farmhouse lab. He had ruined my life. He'd taken everything I'd loved away from me.

"Anna?" Dani called, startling me. I hadn't heard her come in. "Cas and I were just talking about getting something to eat and—"

I hurried over to her and shoved the laptop in her face. "Read this."

"Um. Okay?" She took the computer, holding it up as she read. I knew when she reached the part about Sam by the way she looked at me, the pain in her eyes. "Oh no. I don't...I don't remember this at all...."

"He did it. Sam killed them."

"Maybe there's an explanation."

"No. It's there in the files, and Uncle Will said he did it, and..."

She set the laptop on the floor and took my face in her hands. "If this is true..."

I swallowed the wedge in my throat.

"Where's Nick?" she asked, pulling away.

"He's sleeping in one of the bedrooms last I knew—"

"You have to go."

"What, now?"

"Do you have any idea how dangerous this is? Who knows what else he's capable of? Oh, God. I can't believe he did it."

"Where am I going to go?" I whispered.

"Do you have anyone you trust?"

"No...I mean...my dad, I guess."

"Then call him."

"What about you?" I asked.

She unplugged the flash drive from the laptop and slid it in the pocket of my jeans. "You want my advice, trust no one. Maybe not even me."

"You're my sister," I said, and for the first time, it felt true.

"And as your sister, I'm telling you to go. I'll feel better once you're somewhere safe. Here." She handed me a set of car keys. "It's the blue SUV in the parking lot."

"Where did you—"

"Shh." She glanced toward the bedrooms. "Come on." She led me to the door and scanned the hallway beyond before waving me through.

I grabbed my bag and followed her out.

In the hallway, she gave me a quick hug and a peck on the cheek. "Be safe," she said and urged me into the stairwell, shutting the door behind her before I could respond.

With my heart hammering in my ears, I took the stairs down two at a time and slipped out the rear exit, near the parking lot. I hesitated just outside the door, looking back toward the lobby, wondering if I should tell Nick or Cas, or even Sam, what Dani and I had read.

I didn't want to be alone.

I didn't want to leave.

I'll take my chances, I thought. There had to be an explanation, right?

But then the rational side of my brain kicked in and said that I needed to be strong, that I needed to go.

Inside the SUV, I jammed the key into the ignition. Snow started to fall in fat, lazy flakes that melted when they hit the windshield.

I tugged the car into drive and pulled out of the parking lot.

24

SINCE I'D LEFT THE CELL PHONE BACK
at the condo, I had to go looking for a pay phone. I finally found one
after nearly an hour of driving. And then it took me another ten minutes to find enough quarters in the car to make a call.

Dad answered on the second ring.

"Hello?" he said, his tone guarded.

"Dad. It's me. I don't have a lot of time. I'm on a pay phone."

He breathed out. "If you're calling me from a pay phone," he said,
"I can only assume you're in trouble."

I clutched the phone harder and looked out on the gas station parking lot. The sun was beginning to rise, and morning commuters were
pulling into the parking lot to fill up on gas, coffee, and doughnuts.

This station had a bakery in back, and I could smell the fried dough from all the way out here.

My stomach growled.

"I need to come stay with you for a few days," I said.

"Anna," he said with a quick exhalation, "you know it's not safe, and—"

I couldn't hold the tears in anymore.

They came pouring out. I scrunched my eyes closed as I tried to get control of myself, but it was no use. My breath quivered, and Dad caught on instantly.

"Where are you? Are you still in Michigan?"

"Yes."

"What meeting place are you closest to?"

A week after we'd escaped Branch headquarters, Dad and I had come up with several meeting places around Michigan, and a few across the country, so that we could tell each other where to meet simply by using a code.

You could never be too sure about a secure line, or privacy, for that matter. The man wearing a business suit and bright-red tie hovering at the newspaper stand behind me could very well be a Branch employee.

I had to be careful. Always.

"I'm closest to location four."

Four was code for Millerton, Michigan, just outside Grand Rapids, and Dad and I had agreed to meet at Millerton Park, in the center of town, if location four was ever needed.

I'd never been there before, but I'd consulted the Michigan map when Dad and I came up with the locations. I knew how to get to the park easily enough.

"I'm three and a half hours away," Dad said. "I'll meet you there soon."

I sucked in a breath. "Thanks."

"Just be careful till I get there. Okay?"

"I will."

"And Anna?" he asked. "Are the boys with you?"

I squeezed my eyes shut again and wrapped the phone's cord around my finger. "No. I'm by myself."

Dad sighed, like he'd expected that answer. "I'll see you soon, okay?"

"Hurry, please."

"I will."

I bought a coffee and a cake doughnut from the gas station and then sat in the parking lot, stuffing my face.

Since I didn't want to arrive at location four too soon, I waited around the gas station for at least an hour, then navigated back to the freeway. I arrived at Millerton Park just before nine.

The park was situated in the middle of town and covered a total of five acres. There were at least six different parking lots, so Dad and I had agreed to meet on a park bench near the center, where the fountain was.

I plopped down on a bench, zipping up my coat against the cold. Behind me, the fountain was dry, the base cluttered with trash and dead leaves. The playground just over the next hill was empty.

It seemed to take my dad forever to show, and when he finally did, we stood awkwardly, each waiting for the other to do something. Dad and I weren't the hugging type.

"It's good to see you," he said, stuffing his hands in his coat pockets.

"You, too."

I took a second to look Dad over. He seemed like he'd aged a lot in the weeks since I'd last seen him. There were new wrinkles bursting from the corners of his eyes and new laugh lines hugging his mouth.

"How are you feeling?" I asked.

He shrugged. "I'm feeling all right. And you? You look skinnier. Are you eating well?"

"Yes. I've been running regularly with the boys."

Neither of us acknowledged the reason behind my sudden interest in endurance and physical training. After all, Dad was partially responsible for this new way of life. He'd been a Branch employee for a long time. And he'd headed the program that'd altered the boys and me.

But I didn't blame him. Not really. He'd been doing what he'd thought was right at the time. And he'd helped us when it counted.

He still felt guilty, though. Which was why I mentioned the Branch as little as possible.

"Come on," Dad said, nodding toward the parking lot behind him. "Let's get out of the cold."

I'd planned on ditching Nick's stolen car anyway, so I'd brought my things. Dad led me to a pickup truck. It was indigo, with a few patches of rust and a white pinstripe along both sides.

I climbed in and set my stuff on the floorboard. Dad slid in next to me and started up the truck with a bit of coaxing.

He gave me a smile. "The Branch would never suspect I'd drive an eighty-one Chevy. It's a good cover car."

"I like it."

"You don't have to lie. It smells like stale cigarettes and runs like crap. But it gets the job done."

"That's all that matters."

Dad drove south of town, sticking to back roads. The snow had let up some, but driving conditions weren't the best, and the main streets were a slushy mess.

"You want to tell me what's going on?" Dad finally asked. "Last I heard, I was supposed to be looking into a new brainwashing technique at Sam's request. Now you're alone, and you need my help. Sam wasn't brainwashed, was he?"

"No, at least not that we know."

Dad visibly relaxed. "Well, that's good. I don't know that we'd be strong enough to go up against Sam."

We weren't.

"So, tell me," Dad said.

"I don't even know where to start."

"From the beginning is usually best."

I recounted everything we'd learned. Dad listened while he chewed on a straw. "You suspect Sam killed your parents?" he asked a few minutes later. "That's quite the theory."

"It's not a theory. It was in Sam's files. And my uncle was there, too."

Dad frowned. "Your uncle?"

"Yeah. Why?"

"I don't know." Dad shrugged. "I was told you had no surviving family. I suppose I shouldn't have believed anything Connor told me, but I didn't know you had an uncle out there. If I had . . ."

"It's all right, Dad. Really."

"Yes, well." He let out a sigh. "Anyway." He cleared his throat. "So you think the boys could possibly have been programmed with some kind of new brainwashing technique."

"Yes. Sam told you about the others we found in Delta lab, right?"

"He did."

"We think maybe the Branch programmed Cas and Sam while they were at Branch headquarters a few months ago."

"But"—Dad lifted a finger—"if they'd been brainwashed then, why not activate them during the confrontation at headquarters? Connor could have saved himself a lot of trouble and spared his life if he had. Seems like a waste."

I frowned. "Yeah, good point."

"And to be honest, Anna, I wouldn't believe everything I read in those files. Even if Trev's actions were well-intentioned, that doesn't mean the information is true."

"But how could they have known to plant false information at the time Trev copied the files?"

Dad thought about that one. "I don't know. Has the flash drive been in your possession ever since then? Has it ever been out of your sight?"

"You mean, for someone to add that file?" I asked. Dad nodded. "I'm pretty sure it's been with Sam since we left our last rental house."

"No one has had access to it?"

"Not that I know...well, wait...Greg. Or either of the other two boys from Delta."

"There you have it," Dad said as he slowed for a traffic light.

A small feeling of hope spread through me.

Dad clicked on his blinker. The idling of the truck engine was now the only sound between us.

Something else wasn't right; I just didn't know what it was. I could see the pieces in my head, but I couldn't put them together. I didn't think Greg or the others had had the time to alter the flash drive. And even if they had, they would have been fully conscious at the time.

Greg and the others had seemed grateful for being rescued. And when they were activated, they were completely blank with one sole mission: to take Sam, Nick, and Cas out. Greg had punched Dani, but once she was out of the way, they'd ignored her and gone after the boys.

There was only one other person who had access to the flash drive: Dani. And she'd been the last to speak to Greg. What had she said to him?

It was something odd, not a frequently used word. I remembered that much.

It was...vigilant. *Be vigilant.*

Had Dani activated Greg and the others? Hadn't she tried to get me to leave then? While the boys fought Greg?

"Where's your phone?" I asked.

"Center console."

I dug it out and punched in Sam's number. It rang. And rang and rang and rang.

I ended the call and dialed Nick. No answer there, either.

"Can you turn around?" I said. "We need to go back to Grand Rapids."

Dad glanced across the truck cab. "You sure?"

"Yeah. I just...I need to talk to Sam face-to-face. I should have talked to him in the first place."

At the next intersection, Dad took a left, made a U-turn when the street was clear, and headed in the direction we'd just come from.

As he drove, I went over every conversation I'd had with Dani since we'd found her.

One of the first things we talked about was my relationship with Sam. Nick thought it was odd that Dani hadn't reacted more to the news, but Sam and Dani had been separated for five years.

Nick had said he didn't trust her.

And he had the best gut instinct of anyone I'd ever met.

It seemed to take forever for us to reach the condominium complex. Even longer because I couldn't remember exactly where it was. When we finally pulled into the parking lot and found it empty, I nearly lunged from the vehicle.

"Wait," Dad called, but I couldn't.

I had to see the boys with my own eyes and assure myself that they were all right. That I hadn't just made the stupidest mistake I could ever make.

I'd trusted Dani over Nick, and Sam and Cas.

Dani may have been blood, but I didn't know anything about her.

Nick had warned me, and I'd totally disregarded him.

Inside, I whipped open the entrance to the stairwell. The elevators were inoperable, which meant I had seven whole flights of stairs to run up before I reached the floor where the boys were.

"I can't keep pace with you," Dad shouted as I pulled ahead.

"Meet me on the seventh floor, then. It's unit 722."

I made good time up the stairs and stopped at the door to the seventh floor to peek through the tiny square window. The hallway was dark despite the late-morning hour, and nothing seemed out of place.

With my heart drumming in my ears, I tugged on the door latch and pulled it toward me. It didn't make a sound. I eased into the hallway. Looked left, then right. Still, nothing seemed amiss.

I crept toward 722.

The door was slightly ajar.

I reached for my gun and peered inside, ducking to make myself a smaller target just in case.

There was no movement.

No lights.

Nothing.

I nudged the door with my boot and it creaked open.

Shattered glass glittered on the tile floor. A cupboard door had been ripped off its hinges and lay smashed near the pantry. One of the cast-iron stove burners had been tossed clear across the room.

I froze just inside the door, knowing that once I searched the condo and found it empty, I'd realize they were really gone, that my sister had betrayed me, that I'd trusted the wrong person.

So if I just stood here a minute longer, it wouldn't be true.

Please don't let it be true.

"Nick?" I called out, and my voice seemed to boomerang back at me, as if to say, *Who are you talking to? There's no one here.*

"Sam? Cas?"

Nothing.

Dad entered the condo behind me minutes later. "Oh no," he said.

I rounded the kitchen island, raced down the hallway, checked the rooms, the bathrooms, the closets. Nothing. No one. They weren't here.

I returned to the kitchen to find Dad staring at the stainless steel fridge, at a folded note stuck to the front.

"It's written to you," Dad said, handing it to me.

I opened it and recognized the handwriting immediately.

"It's from Riley," I said. " 'Thank you for your cooperation in this cleanup process. We couldn't have done it without you. Sam, Cas, and Nick fought valiantly until we told them you were already at Branch headquarters. And then they came willingly. It made my job much easier. PS: The word you're looking for is *erased*.' "

I frowned. "What does that mean?"

Dad walked past me and grabbed the cast-iron stove burner off the living room floor. He said nothing as he swiveled around and stared right at me.

"Dad?"

His eyes were blank, unblinking. His mouth was set in a straight line.

There was no emotion at all on his face as he swung the burner at my head.

I ducked. Stood. Ducked for a second attack.

"Dad!"

He cocked his arm back, swung again. I scrambled around the island backward so I could see the next blow when it came. But I tripped over the detached cabinet door and slammed straight down on the floor.

I saw the burner come flying toward me. I realized suddenly where I'd gone wrong.

The Branch hadn't brainwashed a code word into the boys.

They had brainwashed my dad.

25

I FELT THE LULL OF MOVING TIRES
beneath me, but I couldn't seem to open my eyes.

Voices rang in my head, calling me back into a dream or an old memory. I couldn't tell which.

There was a flash of auburn hair, spinning and spinning. And my hair, blond like dry wheat, tangled around my face.

"Fly, bird!" Dani shouted. She let me go, and I sailed through the air, landing with a splash. The water filled in the space around me, and I kicked up toward the surface, breaking through with a deep gasp of air.

Dani laughed. "Was that fun?" she asked.

"That was awesome!" I shouted back, and she laughed again.

Sam appeared behind her, wrapping his arms around her waist, and I stopped smiling. Because she was no longer looking at me. She was looking at him.

Air bubbles rose to the surface two feet away from me, and a second later, Nick popped up. He tossed his head back, like a shaggy dog, and water droplets hit my face.

Cas ran, leapt off an outcropping, and did a cannonball, fanning water over me.

"Cas!" I screeched when he broke through the surface laughing.

"You're such an idiot," Nick said.

"At least I'm a good-looking one!" Cas countered.

I looked to shore. Sam and Dani were gone.

"You think you can make it to that island over there?" Nick asked.

I squinted against the sun as I followed his line of sight. There was a small island several yards off, with a cluster of pine trees and not much else. But I wanted to go, mostly because Nick was challenging me to. And I wanted to show him I could make it.

"Yeah," I said, and started swimming.

Cas pulled ahead of me. "I'll beat you both!" he screeched right before he ducked beneath the water and disappeared out of sight.

I dog-paddled over because I didn't know how to swim any other way. Not like Dani. Or the boys.

Nick swam ahead of me, too, and I paddled faster.

Soon my arms and legs were tired, and the island seemed a lot farther away than it had when I'd sized up the distance.

What if I couldn't make it?

The doubt wedged into my chest, squeezing my lungs, and I started to panic.

I flailed, hands slapping against the water, but it didn't do me any good. I sank beneath the surface, and water filled my mouth.

The lake seemed to press against me. I stretched with my foot, hoping to reach the bottom, but found only empty space.

My legs cramped. My lungs were on fire. I needed air.

I was going to drown.

A hand grabbed me by the wrist and hauled me to the surface.

I sputtered and gasped, drinking in the fresh air like I couldn't get enough of it.

"You okay?" Nick asked, and I latched on to him, arms wrapped tightly around his neck.

"Hey," Nick said. "Climb on my back, and I'll swim to shore. Can you do that?"

I nodded and did as he asked, hanging on to him from behind.

Cas swam up beside me. "You all right, bird?"

No. I wasn't. I felt like crying. "I'm okay," I said, which made Nick snort.

Cas rushed ahead of us so he could help pull me out when Nick reached the shore. Cas sat me beneath a scraggly pine tree, on a bed of rust-orange pine needles. Nick reappeared a second later with his navy sweatshirt and draped it around my shoulders.

"Look at me," Cas said, nudging my chin with his thumb. "Who am I?"

"Cas." My teeth chattered together.

"What day is it?"

"Saturday."

"She almost drowned, you idiot," Nick said. "She didn't get hit by a bus."

"Yeah, which means her brain was starving for oxygen, which means brain damage, dickhead."

"I'm okay," I said again, still shivering.

The boys stared at each other.

"We can't tell Dani what happened," Cas said.

Nick tugged on his T-shirt. "I was thinking the same thing."

I looked up at them hovering over me. "Why?"

"Because she'd kill us," Cas answered, running a towel over his head. His blond hair stuck straight up. "Kill us dead. And then kill us again." He ducked down and ruffled my hair. "There isn't anything she wouldn't do for her little bird," he said.

We stopped moving. I opened my eyes to blinding sunlight and shoved myself to an upright position. Something tightened against me. A seat belt. Country music played softly through the car speakers.

Dani was behind the wheel.

"Hey," she said.

I tensed. "Where are we?"

"You're safe."

"Where's my dad? And the boys?"

"They're safe, too."

My head throbbed just above my left eye, and I reached for the spot, not thinking, and winced when I felt a lump. Old blood came away on my fingers. My stomach rolled, and I had to bite down on my lower lip to stop from barfing.

Concussion, for sure. My dad had given me a concussion.

"Where are we going?" I tried again.

"To a secure location." Dani hit the blinker and turned down a side street.

"Why did you betray us?" I asked, because I needed to distract her while I made a plan.

I had no weapons. I was injured. I had no idea where we were. Or where the boys were.

First I needed information. Then I'd act.

"I didn't betray you," she said, her voice laced with sadness. "I did what I had to do to get you out of there."

She turned left. Warehouses and factories lined the street. Gravel from the snowplows crunched beneath our tires.

"Get me out of where?"

"The Branch." She pulled into a parking lot behind a three-story brick building that said WATCHCASE on the side in old, fading letters.

Windows ran from east to west, some panes of glass smashed or missing.

She stepped out of the vehicle, taking the car keys with her. I scanned the interior, looking for anything I could use as a weapon, but the car was clean.

I fumbled with the door latch and nearly fell out of the vehicle when I managed to open it. Dani was there in an instant, holding me up by the arm.

"Are you all right?" Concern was pressed into the creases of her mouth.

I weighed the possible answers. I could lie and say I was fine, but if I was honest and told her I was in pain, she'd think of me as vulnerable. I could catch her off guard later when the time was right.

With a frown, I fingered the knot on my forehead again. "I don't feel so well."

"I'll get you something when we're inside." She tightened her hold on me as I hunched over. "We're almost there."

She led me around the building to a set of double doors stuck in an alcove. Mint-green paint peeled and curled at the edges. It was unlocked, and we strolled right inside.

"What is this place?" I asked.

"It's a laboratory. I used to work here."

It didn't look like any laboratory I'd ever seen. The hallways were dirt-crusted, the ceilings decorated with cobwebs. Graffiti marked the walls in a rainbow of colors. The place was entirely empty, and the wind whistled through holes in the windows.

"Here," Dani said, steering me toward an office with a door marked ACCOUNTS PAYABLE.

At the door, she tapped a finger against a tiny silver panel, and a screen slid out of the wall. She pressed her entire hand to the glowing green glass, and it scanned her print.

When she passed the verification, the door opened with a hiss, and a man—a fully uniformed agent—stepped out. ·

"Afternoon, Ms. O'Brien," he said, holding the door for us.

I backpedaled. "This is a Branch location?"

Dani looked at me. "It's safe. Come on."

"No. I'm not going inside there with you. I might never come out."

"Cal," Dani said to the agent. "Some assistance."

Cal grabbed my wrist and hauled me inside. Dani shut the false panel and locked it.

The hallway was lit every three feet with white orb lights screwed into the brick wall. But the lights stopped at an elevator bank. The doors stood open, waiting.

I stiffened.

"It'll be all right, bird. I swear it." Dani looked over at me, her expression open, readable. I believed she wouldn't hurt me, at least not physically, but the farther underground I was, the harder it'd be to escape. The hallway here was narrow, and there was no other exit that I could see. The agent had a rifle slung over his back, and a handgun strapped to his hip. He was big enough to bar the doorway with only his body.

"Come on." Dani coaxed me inside.

There was only one button on the control panel, and Dani hit it with her index finger. So the laboratory was down only one level, which meant it probably wasn't too far underground. Maybe there was some kind of return air vent I could access. Or a supply route. They couldn't possibly haul in laboratory equipment through that door.

The elevator doors slid closed, and the car lurched downward.

"What's going to happen to the boys?" I asked.

Dani leveled her shoulders as the elevator came to a stop. "I honestly don't know. Not yet, anyway."

The doors opened with a *ding*, and a bustling laboratory came into view.

I stepped out behind Dani.

There were long work counters near the front, with beakers and microscopes and vials in trays. In the far corner, behind a wall of glass, there were several treadmills with monitors surrounding each one.

A row of computers took up the back of the space, and each station was manned by someone wearing a white lab coat.

It was too clean, too sterile, and gooseflesh rose on my arms.

Dani wound through the place, and everyone we passed stopped to say hello. They called her Ms. O'Brien, like she was someone important.

We passed several desks, where lab technicians were scribbling notes and reading reports and generally looking busy.

A thin, freckled man met us halfway through the lab, his arms burdened with files. "Ms. O'Brien," he said. "You're early."

He wasn't much older than us. Twenty-three, maybe. He tripped over a circuit pad, stumbled forward, kneed the edge of a desk, and gritted his teeth.

"Are you okay?" I asked, and he finally looked at me.

"Oh. It's you." He nodded once, twice, swallowed. "It's a pleasure to finally meet you." He shuffled the files to his other arm and held out his hand. "I'm Brian Lipinski."

I stared at him. I was a prisoner here, wasn't I? I wasn't about to make nice with anyone inside.

"Umm...okay." He pulled his hand back. "No handshakes. That's cool."

Dani snapped her fingers. "Brian."

"Oh. Yes? OB is in the back room waiting for you."

OB. I knew that name from somewhere.

Dani muttered a thank-you and motioned me through a door, down another hallway, and into a small office.

I froze when I saw Uncle Will.

Why was he here? There were no other agents in the room, so it wasn't as if he was being held against his will.

Wait.

All my alarm bells went off.

OB.

The name had been mentioned in one of Dani's files. Something about OB requesting a shift in the time line.

OB. O'Brien.

As in Will O'Brien.

"Oh my God." I staggered back and slammed into the door, fumbling for the knob, and finding none. I turned around, patted at the crack in the door, but nothing happened.

"You didn't give her a sedative yet?" Uncle Will asked.

"No. I wanted to talk to her first."

"Without the sedative, how did you think she would react to seeing me here? You think you can talk to her when she's like this?"

A hand clamped down on my shoulder. I grabbed the wrist, whirled, stomped down with the heel of my boot, pinning Uncle Will's ankle beneath me. I twisted his arm around and up at an unnatural angle. Pain contorted his face.

"Anna," he said. "We just want to talk."

My heart drummed a steady beat in my head. Sweat beaded at the nape of my neck. I tried to control my breathing, like Sam had taught me.

I let Will go, and he eased back.

"Have a seat," he said as he shook out his arm.

I looked at the overstuffed leather chair. This was more an office than it was a medical room. Dark wood bookcases lined the wall to my left. There was a desk in the rear, which Uncle Will had been sitting at when we arrived, and four leather chairs in the center of the room.

"No, thanks." I clasped my hands behind my back, wishing there was a gun there, hidden beneath my shirt. I didn't like how vulnerable I felt without a weapon.

"Very well." Uncle Will crossed his arms over his chest. He wasn't a large man, but not small, either. Maybe six feet and an even build. I was confident I could take him but not confident I could take him *and* Dani. At least not yet.

I needed to know my surroundings better, and their weaknesses And I needed to find the boys.

"So, where should we start?" Uncle Will asked.

"Start with telling me what the hell is going on. Do you work for the Branch?"

Dani sat on the edge of the desk and stretched her legs out in front of her. "You might as well tell her, Uncle Will."

Will gave Dani a look that I couldn't see. When he turned again, to me, his expression was impassive. "I don't *work* for the Branch. I created it."

I let my arms drop to my sides. "You what?"

"Which makes us princesses of the castle," Dani said, but she almost sounded sad, more like she thought it a curse than anything else.

My ears rung with the words. How could my own family have

created this nightmare? How could Riley and Connor not be the worst of it?

"But your men have shot at me. I've almost died multiple times."

Will held up his hand. "Your life was never in danger. I made sure my men knew that. And if I hear otherwise, those agents will be dealt with accordingly."

I shook my head. "I can't be a part of this place. I care about the boys. And I want to be left alone."

Will shook his head. "I can't allow that. I'm sorry."

"I made a deal," Dani said. She rose to her feet and came over to me. Her eyes were watery. I held my breath as I waited to hear what deal she'd made. "Everything I do, everything I've always done, is for you." She pressed her lips together, inhaled through her nose, her shoulders rising an inch, like she was bracing herself for my reaction. "You and me, our freedom, in exchange for the boys."

Dread scuttled down my spine and a hollow pit opened in my gut. "No." I shook my head. "No."

She tilted her head aside. "I've already made the deal, bird."

My teeth ground together and I tightened my hands into fists. "We still have the files Sam took years ago, with the kill sheets and the lab logs and—"

Will cut me off. "I know, which is why you're here."

"What do you—" Realization swept in. They were going to use me as a bargaining chip against Sam, to make him give up the files.

And he might just do it.

But there was no way Will was going to let the boys and me go. Our freedom wasn't a price he was willing to pay in exchange for the files.

I turned to Dani. "I'll never forgive you for this. I won't." My hands tightened into fists. "I will hunt you down until you are dead, and you'll stay dead this time."

The door burst open behind me. An agent marched in, a rifle slung over his back. Behind him was a second man, a face I knew. Greg.

"Greg," I said, hesitating. "It's Anna. Are you..." I wanted to say, *Are you in there?* But that seemed a silly thing to say.

"Don't bother," Dani said. "He's been activated, and he'll stay that way until he's fulfilled his mission."

I licked my lips. "Which is?"

"To kill Sam, Nick, and Cas," Will answered as he opened an unmarked door in the far wall. "Call me when they arrive," he said.

Greg and the other agent hooked their arms beneath mine and hauled me off my feet. I kicked, flailed. "No! Greg! Please listen to me."

"This will all be over soon," Dani promised. She sniffed, wiped her nose with the back of her hand. "By this time tomorrow, you won't remember a thing. It'll be like we've never even been separated."

The two men carried me out the door. I kicked the agent on my left, then Greg on my right, but I couldn't get enough momentum to do any damage.

We went down a hallway where I was eventually tossed into a tiny room. The door was shut and a lock slid into place. I pounded on it for as long as I could, until I was exhausted and my hands were numb.

I slumped on the bed shoved into the corner and cried until I fell asleep.

26

I WAS NUDGED AWAKE SOME TIME later. Still groggy, eyes heavy, I had a hard time seeing who it was at first. I sat up. Scrubbed the sleep from my eyes and looked again.

Riley.

"Morning," he said. "We have a job for you." He waved his fingers, and two new agents came into the room.

"What kind of job?" I asked.

No one answered.

I was dragged from my room. Riley led us down the hallway. I hadn't eaten in what felt like forever, which left me too exhausted to fight. And judging by the thickness of my tongue, the dryness of my mouth, I was bordering on dehydration.

After several more twists and turns, Riley finally stopped at a steel door, unlocked it with a key card, and let it swing open. The room was gray brick, the floor the same. There was one metal folding chair in the center.

The agents dragged me inside, and it wasn't until I was past the door that I realized the room wasn't empty.

Sam was chained to the ceiling at the far end, his arms held above his head, shackles tight around his wrists. When he saw me, the chains rattled as every muscle in his body tensed. He was shirtless, barefoot, in nothing but black pants.

Bruises peppered his torso, his arms, his face. A gash on his cheek was crusted over with blood.

They were going to torture him in front of me, weren't they? Get me to give up the files. Or maybe the flash drive.

I was worried it would work, too. I was worried I wouldn't put up a fight at all and Sam would know how much of a coward I was.

The agents pushed me into the metal folding chair. My hands were cuffed behind the back, my legs tied to the chair's legs. The whole time, I didn't take my eyes off Sam and he didn't take his eyes off me.

We could get through this. Couldn't we?

I'm sorry, I mouthed.

This was my fault.

Because I'd doubted him.

Because I'd believed all the wrong things and all the wrong people.

I tried to prepare myself for whatever was about to happen. Tried telling myself Sam was strong, that he could get through a lot of pain, that he wouldn't want me to give in so easily.

I can do this, I thought.

And that's when the first blow came.

It was a straight shot of a tightened fist aimed expertly at my jaw.

My chair teetered back on its legs. My teeth slammed together and the pain throbbed down to the roots, through my bones.

It wasn't Sam they were torturing. It was me.

Another blow to the ribs. Another to the stomach. Something cracked. Chains rattled. I couldn't see straight. Blood filled my mouth.

A boot to the head. My chair tipped over sideways, and my swollen cheek pressed against the ice-cold concrete floor.

"Stop!" Sam said. His chains rattled again. "Please."

"I need the location of the files," Riley said. "Every single copy. Any preplanned media spread, I want details on those, too."

Sam didn't say anything at first. My chair was righted. I blinked back the tears in my eyes and managed to see Sam's face through the grimy haze.

Don't do it, I thought.

An arm snaked around my neck. A blade was pressed into my throat.

"Come on, Sam," Riley said, "or she bleeds out in front of you."

I didn't think they'd do it. Did Sam know that my uncle was the one who ran the Branch? Riley wouldn't kill me, would he?

The blade cut into my skin, slowly, carefully.

I cried out. A trail of blood ran down my neck.

"Okay." Sam struggled against his cuffs. His teeth were clenched so tight, I worried they'd break. "I'll give you whatever you want."

"Good," Riley said behind me. "Good."

And then I was dragged from the room.

I passed out not long after I left Sam and woke sometime later with a cold rag on my face. I shrank away when I saw it was Dani who was cleaning my wounds. "Hey," she said. "You're okay. I'm just cleaning you up."

I was back in my little cell, lying flat on my bed. "I'm sorry," Dani said.

"Don't touch me." I slapped her hand away.

She frowned. "It wasn't my idea, torturing you. Riley is...well... you know how Riley is."

Everything hurt. My head was pounding. My teeth felt crooked, as if they'd been smashed together with that kick to the face. There was something wet sliding down my nose. Dani wiped it away, and the rag came back covered in blood.

"Nothing is broken," she said. "I had you checked."

"Wow. Thanks for that."

She sighed. "I really am sorry."

"You keep saying that."

"And it'll never be enough."

"I want Sam," I said, my voice cracking, revealing all the fear I was trying to keep locked away. Was he dead already? Had Riley let Greg finish his mission?

Dani reached over and pushed a strand of hair behind my ear. "You can't have him, bird."

The door opened again and Dani stepped back. Greg and his partner tugged me off the bed.

"Careful with her," Dani warned.

This time, I didn't fight.

I was taken to a different room where two white-coated technicians readied an array of machines. Wires and electrodes were splayed out on two stainless steel trays, and I was thrust into the cushy leather chair in the middle of them. Greg tightened a strap around my upper body, locking me in place. He wasn't acknowledging me, or speaking at all, so that gave me some hope. He hadn't completed his mission yet, otherwise he would be back to normal.

A technician shoved a rubber guard into my mouth.

Dani came over and nudged my chin up with her index finger, forcing me to look at her. "It'll be over soon." She leaned in, her hair swinging off her shoulders. "I love you," she whispered, then kissed my forehead, just as I wound my fingers in her hair and gave it a hard tug.

27

CAUGHT OFF GUARD, DANI DIDN'T FIGHT
back right away.

I bucked up, slamming a knee into her head. Once, twice. She
staggered. The technicians pressed themselves into the corner. The
other agent started for me. I lashed out at the last second, tripping
him with a foot. He pitched forward into my lap, and I snagged the
knife from his gear belt.

Dani punched me. The chair rocked to the side.

It wasn't bolted down.

She punched me again, and I aided the momentum, pushing
with my feet so that I rocked to the right and tipped over.

"Sedate her," she said, and the technicians sprang to life.

I sawed at the strap on my right arm, the one hidden from view.

I could hear the shuffle of the agent's boots, but couldn't see him yet around the base of the chair.

Hurry. Damn it.

I nicked myself with the knife, and sharp pain burned from the wound.

The agent wrapped his hands around my arm and lifted me upright just as the strap frayed on its last threads and finally came loose. I swung with everything I had and landed a solid punch to the man's face. He fell back and whacked his head on the metal base of a medical machine.

Greg came for me next. I dug the toes of my boots into the floor and thrust forward with the knife, stabbing him in the chest.

The blond technician gasped and scrambled for the door, her coworker right behind.

Greg dropped at my feet.

Dani and I stared at each other.

"What do you plan to do, Anna?" she asked. "Kill me? You won't make it out of here, not without help. And then what? Rescue the boys? They're just boys!" She edged closer. "We are *blood*. Sisters."

"I don't even know you!" I shouted.

She shrank back. The look on her face, of pure heart-wrenching sadness, softened my resolve.

To her, I was the little sister who needed to be saved. A child, still. Someone bargained for, not *with*.

But to me, she was just a stranger, and I suspected that hurt worse than any physical blow.

She gritted her teeth. "I can't lose you again. I just can't." She pulled a gun from beneath her sweater and pointed it at me. "Drop the knife."

I stalled to weigh my options.

"Drop the knife!"

I did. It clattered on the floor.

Dani eased toward me. "If there were a way for me to make you remember," she started, "I'd do it. It would be so much easier. Trust me. You would see..."

"What?" I raised my arms, annoyed. "What would I see?"

"That our parents were shitty parents. That *I* was the one who took care of you. That everything I've done, I've done for you!"

"Like give away the boys? I don't want that. They deserve their freedom more than any of us."

She laughed. "Oh, because Sam is so innocent?"

"He didn't kill our parents, did he? For all I know, you were the one who killed them."

"No." She shook her head for emphasis. "We lied to protect you."

I snorted. "I'm sure."

"I lied about something else, too. I *was* there that night, the night our parents died."

I tilted my head, caught off guard. "You were?"

"But I wasn't the one who killed our parents. It was you."

28

I FROWNED. "YOU EXPECT ME TO BELIEVE that? I was just a kid. I loved them."

"You've been having flashbacks, haven't you? To that night? Sam said you were. And your flashbacks have been more debilitating than Nick's and Cas's, haven't they? More severe? It's because you've gone through more memory alterations than the others."

I faltered. "You mean, at the farmhouse?"

"No." She shook her head. "Before then. When you were younger."

I snorted. "You're trying to tell me our parents didn't notice their daughter coming home with no memories?"

"The Branch had just developed the ability to wipe memories and plant whatever they wanted in the voids. You were the first to receive them. And more than once."

A lump wedged itself in the center of my throat, and no amount of swallowing seemed to dislodge it. Because I worried she was telling the truth.

"Why would they do that?" I asked.

"I think you already know the answer."

The flashback I'd had a few days ago came back to me. In it, Dani had asked if our dad had hit me. She'd instantly gone on alert.

He hadn't, though. Had he? I'd said no.

But even if he had, that didn't explain why I would have killed him and our mother.

"I don't believe you," I said.

"I didn't expect you would."

Someone grabbed me from behind. Two hands on my left arm. Two hands on my right. The lab techs. They swung me around, dragging me toward the chair. I wrenched my right arm out of the woman's grip and socked her with my elbow. Blood spurted out her nose, and she slammed into the wall.

The man was harder to slip. Once he saw his partner go down, he tightened his hold, bracing his feet. So I punched him in the face and followed it with an elbow to the same spot. His eyes rolled back, and he slumped to the ground.

I scooped up the knife and turned just in time to see the stainless steel medical tray whack me across the head. I stumbled. The coppery taste of blood ran down my throat.

Dani swung the tray again, but I ducked and thrust upward with the knife. Dani collapsed in my arms. I stumbled back from her weight.

She coughed, and her lips came away red. "Bird," she said, "it wasn't supposed to be like this."

I'd kept it together this whole time. Kept the tears down. The emotion locked in a place I didn't want to touch. But it all came pouring out at once.

"I didn't...I didn't mean..." I sputtered.

Dani's legs buckled, and I eased her to the floor. The knife was lodged somewhere between her sternum and stomach. Her sweater was heavy and wet with blood.

"I'm sorry," I said, pushing the hair from her face. "I'll get someone. Someone can help you."

She wrapped her tiny hand around my wrist. "No." Her breath scraped down her throat. It sounded alien, unnatural. "You're all I have left...." Tears streamed down her face. "I've lived my entire life trying to protect you." She laughed, and it quickly turned into long, racking coughs. "You clearly don't need me anymore."

I took her face in my hands and forced her to look at me. Her eyes lost focus. It was like she was looking straight through me.

"We can fix this. Tell me where the boys are. Where would they take them?"

She shook her head.

"Please." Desperate, I threw in one more promise. "We can run together. All of us."

"Even Nick?" She smiled. "I made you that same promise once, and that's what you asked for. You asked for him to come with us."

She shuddered. "There was always something about him. You should know that. That's why you did it, I think. To protect him." She laughed, but there was no humor in her tone. "The first time you went through a memory alteration, I got called away at the last second, and Nick was there when you woke. He was always there, every time after that."

"Dani, please—"

"You know how they say a baby bird shouldn't be handled by humans too soon after birth for fear of the bird becoming attached to the human?"

"Yeah, I've heard of that."

"I always told Sam that's what happened with you and Nick. The first time your memories were tampered with, it was like you were reborn, and Nick was the first person you saw. Sam thought I was crazy, but…" She closed her eyes and several tears ran down her cheeks. "I should have been there when you woke up. I never should have left you alone with Mom and Dad to begin with. I should have been with you every second of every single day."

I grabbed her shoulders. "None of that matters to me now. Just tell me where the boys are. Please?"

She opened her eyes and finally looked at me. "I can't. Uncle Will won't come after you if he has the boys. You should go. But there is . . ."

The tendons in her neck went rigid as she struggled for another breath.

I shook her. "Dani?"

Nothing. No response. Her eyes were vacant, unblinking, and the room took on an eerie stillness.

"Dani!" She was limp weight in my hands, and her head flopped to the side.

"Where are they?" I screamed.

Only the echo of my voice bouncing off the walls answered back.

I shakily rose to my feet. One of the techs stirred.

I had to get out of here before they woke up. I was exhausted and bruised and broken. I didn't know how much fight I had left in me.

Probably not enough.

I spied the agent's gun on the floor near his body. I scooped it up, checked the clip.

I had just started for the door when it burst open and agents flooded the room.

Suddenly I was surrounded, with a dozen guns trained on me.

"Put the gun on the floor," Riley said from the center of the pack. I eased the gun down. "Thank you," he said. "Now shoot her."

Someone pulled the trigger, and a dart hit me in the chest. I had only enough time to think I was totally screwed before a woozy feeling swept over me and my legs gave out.

29

"What did you do to her?"

I clutched harder at Dani's hand as the woman with blond hair peered down at me. "Is she high?"

"No, Mom," Dani said. "She's just tired."

Mom. This woman was our mother. Yes, I knew that. And the man looming behind her, the man with the straight-edged shoulders and the coppery hair and the slash for a mouth was our father.

Everything felt so disjointed. Like I was stuck in a dream where I knew these were my parents but they didn't fit the image of my parents.

"I'm packing her a bag," Dani went on. "We're taking her for a few days, if that's all right."

Dad stomped over to us and yanked me out of Dani's grip, his fingers tight around my wrist, so tight that I worried my bones might snap beneath the pressure. "You're not taking her anywhere. You think I don't know what you're up to? Will called, you know." He looked past Dani at the boys lined up behind us. "You've gotten my oldest in a hell of a lot of trouble, and you're not taking my youngest with you, too." Air wheezed out of his nose as he clamped his mouth shut and seethed.

"I'm taking her," Dani said again.

Dad shook his head. "No. You're. Not."

I didn't know whose side I should be on. I wanted to go with my sister and with Nick. I knew that much. But if they were in trouble like Dad said, I wasn't so sure.

I looked over my shoulder and met Nick's stare. I always thought his eyes were the color of my sky-blue crayon, the one called ice. It was a color that meant strength to me, indestructible.

If he was going, then I wanted to go, too.

I tugged my arm out of Dad's grip and crossed the room, stopping at Nick's side. I fitted my hand in his. He squeezed just enough to be reassuring.

Dad turned fire-engine red. "I'm calling Will," he said, and his boots thudded into the kitchen.

"Wait!" Mom called.

Sam and Cas started after Dad.

"Get Anna out of here," Dani said.

Nick pulled me down the hallway and into my room, past the four-poster bed and then the dresser. He grabbed my backpack off the hook on my closet door and shoved clothes inside. "Take this," he said, sliding it over my shoulder. He yanked the closet door open and gave me a nudge.

"Wait here. Lock the door." He pointed at the dead bolt that'd been installed on the inside of the closet.

"Don't come out for anything," Nick ordered. "I don't care what you hear. I'll come get you soon."

"You promise?"

"I promise." He shut the door, and I immediately clicked the lock in place.

There was a flashlight somewhere in here. I knew that much. I rooted around on the wood floor until my fingers grazed the edge of a box. Inside I felt paper and something glossy, something hard, like rock, and a flashlight.

I clicked it on and breathed out with relief as the closet filled with a soft golden glow.

Shouting sounded from the front of the house. I cowered in the corner, legs tucked up to my chest. I looked inside the box now that I could see.

There was a picture of Dani and me. A necklace. A smooth stone, like a rubbing stone. A handful of coins. And a flattened paper crane.

I pulled the crane out and puffed up his body.

Nick had made it. The errant thought came to me suddenly, completely, in a way that felt more real than anything had since I'd woken in some medical office with a headache and wires stuck all over my head.

Nick had been there. He'd been the first person I'd seen after opening my eyes, and he'd immediately seemed familiar.

I'd lunged at him, wrapping my arms around his neck. He smelled like oatmeal and coffee and brown sugar and soap. And his return hug was enough to tell me my jumbled mind hadn't been wrong about him.

"It's all right," he said, patting my back awkwardly. "Things will be confusing for a few hours. It'll come back."

"Where am I?" I'd asked. I'd nearly said, *Who am I?* But the name Anna came to mind. "Is something wrong with me?"

"Temporary amnesia," Nick said. "Leaves you feeling like shit, but you'll be okay."

"You've had amnesia before?" I'd asked.

Nick just stared at me, and I quickly realized he hadn't meant "you" in the general, second-person sense. He'd meant me. That I'd gone through temporary amnesia before, and it left me feeling like crap.

"Am I sick?" I'd asked, which made Nick smile.

"No, bird. You're fine."

Bird. That was familiar, too.

Still crouched in the closet, I twirled the paper crane by its points between my fingers.

More shouting sounded from the foyer. Something crashed to the floor. Nick cursed. Dani screamed. I wanted to see what was happening. I didn't want to cower in the closet and wait for it to be over.

I wanted to be sure they were all right.

The lock clicked loudly when I opened it, and I waited a second to see if anyone had heard. But they hadn't. I pushed the door open enough to slip through and tiptoe down the hallway. I peeked around the wall into the foyer.

Dani, Nick, Sam, and Cas were lined up with their backs to me, their hands in the air. Dad had a gun trained on them, but there was another man. He had a gun, too. Someone who I thought I knew, but whose name I couldn't remember. He was tall, blond, pretty in a way I'd never seen in person.

Like a movie star, I thought, and when he smiled, a chill of fear shuddered down my back.

"Where is it?" the blond man said, that bright smile still in place. "Tell me where you stuck the documents you stole, and you can go and take little Anna with you."

Dad blinked and looked at the man, dropping the gun at his side. "No, they can't. They're not taking my daughter!"

The man turned to Dad. "Shut up, Charles."

Dad shook with rage. "I'm not one of your trained monkeys, Connor. You can't boss me around."

The man—Connor—said, "Oh, can't I? What exactly do you plan to do to me? Maybe slap me around a little? Give me a good shake? Maybe slam my head into the wall?"

Dad flinched.

"Let me remind you exactly who I am. I'm not your wife. I'm not your daughter. And you can't outfight me. So shut your goddamn mouth, Charles, and take a step back. I'll handle this."

Connor delivered the entire speech through gritted teeth, but with the smile still plastered on his face.

Which made Dad even madder.

He lunged at Connor, brandishing the gun like a club. He threw a backhanded swing, but Connor ducked and landed a solid blow to Dad's side. Dad keeled over and lost the gun. It clattered to the floor. Mom and Dani both dove for it, but Mom was faster.

Dani recovered, putting herself in a balanced crouch. She swiped a leg at our mother. Mom landed hard on her butt, the gun still clutched in her hand. She pointed it at Dani, but Cas swooped in and punched her.

The gun went off.

I gasped.

Nick clutched at his gut, and Sam caught him as he stumbled.

No. No. Not Nick.

I raced down the hallway, rounded into the bathroom, not bothering to flick on the light. I climbed on the closed toilet seat and, with a grunt, pulled off the tank lid. I saw the outline of a plastic zipper bag submerged in the water. I plunged my hand in, gasping at the cold.

When I pulled the bag out, into the light spilling in from the hallway, I saw the barrel of the gun Dani had hidden there. She'd told me where it was, in case I ever needed it. I didn't know how I remembered that, but I did. And I remembered her teaching me how to use it.

I pulled the gun out, dropped the bag. Double-checked the clip to make sure it was full of bullets.

I hurried down the hallway. My feet weren't moving fast enough.

Nick was lying on the floor, outlined in a pool of blood. Cas was having a hard time standing upright and blood poured from a deep split on his forehead. Sam was on top of Connor, strangling him with his hands until he finally passed out.

And Dad was pointing a gun at Dani.

"What happened to you?" Dad said. "You grew up into nothing but a little bitch."

I brought my arms up, the gun clutched in both my hands.

It didn't take Dad long to notice. He swiveled around, training his gun on me. "And you're turning out just like your sister."

I pulled the trigger. Dad staggered back from the hit and sank to his knees. Mom screamed. She barreled toward me.

She looked like a wild thing, like a ghost or a monster or both, with pale skin and hollow eyes and a mouth twisted in a way that was anything but human.

I shot again.

My breath came too quickly. I squeezed my eyes shut and heard Dad swear beneath his breath.

I thought it was over.

I thought we had won.

"No!" Dani yelled.

Another shot sounded. I opened my eyes the very second the bullet hit me and slammed me to the floor.

"You asshole!" Dani screeched.

My side was suddenly on fire, soaked, sticky and warm with blood. I tried sitting up, but I couldn't seem to move my legs to get enough leverage.

Dani scrambled to my side. "No. No. Anna." Her hands hovered over me like she was afraid to touch me. "Can you hear me, bird?"

"Yeah."

"Can you see me?"

I rolled my head toward her voice but was having a hard time making out her face. "Is he dead?" I asked. I was afraid he'd shoot me again. Or someone else. Like Dani.

"Yes. I think so. Cas, will you check him?"

There was a shuffling of feet. Cas said, "No pulse."

The house was suddenly silent.

Dani took in a breath and pressed her hand against my side. The pain was a flash of light in my head and in my eyes. It hurt so bad I couldn't summon enough energy to scream.

"Call Will," Dani said.

"Do you have any idea what he'll do—" Sam started.

"Call him!" She pressed her face against my chest. I could feel her breath on my neck. It helped root me in my body. "It'll be okay. I swear it. Uncle Will is gonna fix you."

And Nick? Who was going to fix him?

"I can carry her," Sam tried one more time. "Cas can get Nick. We can make it out of here."

Dani shook her head. "She'll die before we're able to get her somewhere safe. And even then...no one has the medical technology that the Branch does."

Was she talking about me? Was I going to die?

"Will is family," she said, her voice a buzz in my ears.

The floor creaked. "You're going to make a deal with him, aren't you?" Sam asked.

"I don't have any other choice."

Sam sighed.

"She's my sister," Dani added.

"Cas, get Will on the phone," Sam said.

"Got it."

Sam crouched by my side. He pushed the hair away from my face, his fingers gentle as he coaxed me to look at him. "She's losing a lot of blood. And her vision is unfocused."

"I know."

"She might not—"

"Don't." Dani squeezed my hand in hers. "Don't."

Cas flipped his phone closed, dropped it on the floor, and smashed it with his boot. "Douche bag is on his way."

"You should go," Dani said. Sam hesitated only long enough for Dani to clench her teeth and yell at him. "Go, Sam!"

"Call me when you have an update." He knelt by Nick, grabbed one arm, and hoisted him over his shoulder. Nick groaned.

"Be safe," Sam said.

Dani nodded as the front door creaked open and closed a second later.

"Anna?" she whispered. She didn't wait for my reply. "Listen. When Uncle Will gets here, let me do the talking, okay? Don't say anything. I'll fix this. I promise."

Connor started moving in the corner.

"Everything's going to be all right." Dani smiled and ruffled my hair. The pain was fading. Maybe I was okay after all.

Connor sat up. "What..." he croaked, before pulling out his phone. "Get me backup. I want a perimeter set up around Port Cadia and get out APBs...."

Dani put a hand on the side of my face, forcing me to look at her. Her eyes were bloodshot and bruised, but I could see my sister, more than anything else. I did feel something for her. Love and admiration. I felt safe here next to her.

"I'll do whatever it takes, bird," she said. "Always."

30

I KILLED MY PARENTS.

It was the first thought to come to me upon waking.

Followed by a sadness and desolation so complete I worried it was now part of my DNA, a virus of guilt I'd carry around with me forever.

The second thought to come to me was that I had been shot five years ago.

I sat up and lifted my shirt. My stomach was devoid of any imperfections. No scars. No puckering of the skin. Nothing.

A breath eased out past my lips. Maybe it wasn't a flashback. Maybe it was a nightmare.

But deep down, I knew I was just making excuses.

I killed my parents.

I was shot.

"You were legally dead for three minutes."

I sat up too fast at the sound of the voice behind me and instantly regretted it. My skull pounded on all sides, and I covered my face with my hands, wincing, as I set my feet to the floor.

"You're safe here," Will said. "Relax."

Sensing his movements, I forced myself to focus. I couldn't let him out of my sight.

"If I was dead," I said, "how did you save me?"

He came around the couch and sat at the far end, elbows on his knees, hands folded together. His shirt was rumpled, his sleeves unbuttoned and rolled back.

"I have the best medical team in the state," he said, "and yet, when I saw you there on the lab table, I worried not even they could bring you back."

I met his eyes and tried to ignore the sadness etched into the fine lines.

"But they did," I said.

He nodded. "They were able to stabilize you and stop the bleeding. Afterward, I had them repair the scar so that it looked as though it were never there in the first place. I didn't want you carrying around that reminder that your own father had shot you."

I swallowed against the lump forming in my throat. Was he telling me more lies? Stories made up to make him seem like the good guy?

That's what I wanted to believe, because it was easier to see Uncle Will in only shades of black. But the flashback seemed real, as real as any of the others.

And more than that, it felt like a missing piece finally clicking into place.

"You should have something to drink." Will nodded at the coffee table in front of me. There was a bottle of water there, along with a packet of crackers and a bottle of ibuprofen.

I eyed the offerings suspiciously.

"I have no reason to drug you," Will said. "You're already here."

As I first nibbled on the crackers, I took the time to scan my surroundings.

I was in a loft. Vents ran across the high ceiling. In front of me were several bookshelves made of rusted pipes and worn wood. They were the kind of thing that looked old but were probably made last year and cost several thousand dollars.

The couch I was on was twice the size of any normal couch. It was upholstered in a dark green velvet, so dark as to almost be black. The floor was stained concrete.

Leaded-glass windows looked out on a span of woods. Nothing distinct enough to tell me where I was.

I took a drink of water, then shook out three pills from the bottle into my palm.

An image flashed in my head. Of Dani. Of her blood on my hands.

She was dead. I killed my mother, my father, my sister.

What kind of person kills their whole family?

Was I a psychopath?

"Where are the boys?" I asked.

Will stared at me for the longest time, and it struck me then how sharp and angled his face was, like a fox's. "You killed Dani," he said finally. All of the emotion had left his eyes.

It made him so much more frightening.

"Where are the boys?" I repeated.

"Do you have any idea how much trouble you've caused?"

"If you had left us alone, there wouldn't have been a problem."

The telltale twitch of a smile appeared at the corners of his mouth. He unrolled his sleeves. "I can't move forward when the past is out there, threatening to ruin everything I've worked for."

"We weren't threatening you. We were just trying to live our lives."

"Which I gave you."

It was true. In some twisted way, I owed everything I was and everyone I knew to this man. Did that give him the right to take it all away?

"Do you want to know how you ended up in the Altered program?" he asked.

I swallowed. Yes. But I didn't want to admit it to him.

"I was shot," I said. That seemed like a good place to start. "And Dani made a deal with you to save me."

"She did."

My pulse crept to a nervous beat. I suspected I already knew the answer to the question I was about to ask. But I didn't want it to be true. "What was the price?"

He steepled his fingers. "Sam and the others."

Even if I'd known that was the answer, it didn't make it less painful hearing it.

Dani had set them up. The boys. That's how they were eventually captured.

"And me?" I said.

"Dani and I decided you were better off in a stable home with someone who could look after you."

"The farmhouse."

"Yes."

"And while I was there, why not make me part of the program?"

"You were only supposed to be part of the testing. You were never supposed to take part in the action."

I glanced away, bit at my lower lip. I wanted to be mad. I *wanted* to hate him.

"Now you and I are all that remain of the O'Briens." He rose to his feet and dug inside a cigar box.

Because of me, I thought, but I couldn't focus on that now. Later. When I was safe I'd deal with the despair and the guilt and the sadness. For now I had to concentrate on escaping.

With Will's back to me, I checked my surroundings again. I needed to find a weapon. There was a metal spherical statue on the bookcase on the far right, and straight through the middle of it was an arrow.

If I remembered correctly, it was called an armillary. It would suffice as a weapon.

Will turned, a cigar tucked in the crook of his bent index finger. He flicked the wheel on a lighter and lit the cut end of the cigar. The air instantly smelled of sweet tobacco.

"So now what?" I asked. "What about the boys? Me?"

"The whole reason Dani and I began this mission was to free you from this life."

I scooted forward on the edge of the couch. "You what?"

"We had to be careful, obviously." He puffed on his cigar, blew the smoke out in a rush. "We knew the boys would never let you go without a fight, and sadly, the Branch was good at what we did, at turning biotechnology into weaponry. We made the boys smarter, stronger, faster. The only way to get to them was through you."

"But why?" I curled my fingers into fists. "If you only wanted me, why go after them at all?"

Will furrowed his brow. "Did you not just hear me say the boys would never let you go? Even if I'd spared them and wiped their memories, they would remember eventually. And we'd be back where we are now. I can't run a business like this." He raised his hands up, exasperated, only to let them drop. "It took me over a decade to build this company. We started as a small weapons design firm, and from there I made the Branch into one of the leading dealers in bioweapons."

He shook his head. "And it was my mistake, mixing family with work. I never should have gone down that road. It made me vulnerable, and it made you a victim. For that I apologize."

I tried to process everything he was saying, but something stuck out in my head. Something I couldn't let go. "You said, 'if I'd spared them.' About the boys."

Will turned to me. "That's right."

My throat constricted. "Past tense."

"I—" He was cut off by the ringing of a phone from somewhere in the loft.

"Excuse me." He disappeared into another room, leaving the question unanswered between us.

Anger became my fuel. I took the opening, tiptoeing over to the bookcase and snatching the armillary from its shelf. I went to the doorway Will had gone through and pressed my back against the wall, cocking the statue over a shoulder so the first thing that hit when I swung was the pointed end of the arrow.

Will's voice was a discreet murmur. "They what?" he said in a tone that was less questioning than it was irritatingly shocked.

I tightened my grip.

"Find who helped them escape and bring them to me. Do you understand?"

Had Sam and the others escaped? Was that who he was talking about?

Hope fluttered in my chest.

"Trev," Will said with a sigh, "I thought I told you to keep your eye on him." Another pause. "That's because he's a goddamn trained assassin! When I gave you the orders, I meant put a team on him and make sure he doesn't come within a hundred feet of Samuel!"

He blew out a breath. "Well, then find them."

The phone was slammed down on a counter.

I pressed my bare feet firmly into the floor, trying to get as much force as I could.

Will started back toward the living room. I braced myself, counted to three, and swung.

Will caught the armillary with his left hand, grabbed my throat with his right, and shoved me into the wall.

I gasped for air.

He wrenched the statue out of my grip and tossed it to the side. It left a gouge in the floor and nearly knocked over a tall vase.

"Now listen," he started. This close, I noticed that not all of the marks on his face were freckles. Some of them were scars, tiny dots of discolored skin, like old burn marks. "We can do this the easy way— you cooperate and come with me, no fighting—or the hard way. Are we clear?"

"Yes." I would take the easy way only until I found another opportunity to escape.

"Good." He let me go. "Then we're leaving. You will find shoes and a jacket on the hook behind the couch."

As I tied my shoes, Will produced another cell phone from his pocket and dialed a number. "Ready the jet," he said. "I'll be there in less than a half hour."

"Jet?" I muttered.

"I'm taking you out of the country until this thing with Sam blows over."

He said *this thing with Sam* as if it were nothing more than an argument over who left out the milk.

I steeled myself. "I'm not leaving the country."

"Yes, you are. You'll be safe there. I'll have someone tend to your injuries."

"I'm not going."

"You are."

We had a silent standoff. His threat loomed over me. Now was not the time to argue.

"Will you wipe my memory?" I asked.

The center of his brow clenched with sadness. His voice cracked when he spoke. "It's for the best."

Of course he thought it was. He and Dani. They thought they'd wipe the slate clean with a memory alteration, as if that would fix everything forever.

It wouldn't.

I couldn't let him put me on that plane.

31

WILL HAD A CAR MEET US IN FRONT
of his place. Wherever we were, we were completely surrounded by
woods. He'd moved me from the warehouse laboratory. Which
meant the boys could be anywhere by now.

Would they reach me before Will reached the plane?

And where was Trev?

"Buckle your seat belt," Will ordered as an agent drove down the
long, winding driveway.

"Which way would you like me to take?" the agent asked.

"The freeway. It'll be harder to spot us in traffic."

In order to reach the freeway, we crossed through some nameless
town. There were only a few cars on the roads, which made me wonder absently what time it was.

"Where exactly are we going?" I asked.

"Europe," Will answered.

"What's in Europe?"

He smiled when he turned to me. "Are you fishing?"

I was.

A traffic light flicked to red, and the agent slowed to a stop. The idling engine was the only sound in the vehicle. Will kept ducking just enough to check the rearview mirror and the scene outside the tinted windows.

"Did the second unit do a sweep?" Will asked the driver.

"They did. Found nothing. No sign of them."

The boys. He had to be talking about the boys.

I had to come up with a plan, and quickly. I could open the door while the car was in motion and leap out. I'd escape injury-free if I rolled properly. But could I outrun Will and his agents?

I might have an opening while we boarded the plane, unless we went to a proper airport. Security would make it nearly impossible to escape without a scene.

And even if it was a smaller, private airport, I'd have nowhere to hide when I ran.

Jumping from the vehicle was my best option.

We drove through several more intersections, hitting all the green lights, and then turned right onto Brennon Street.

The next light was red. We squeaked to a stop.

I tensed every muscle in my body as I anticipated making my move.

The driver pressed a finger to the device in his ear.

I relaxed enough to focus on his words.

"Where?" he said quietly. Then, "Copy."

He whipped the wheel around, performing a U-turn in the middle of the street.

"What is it?" Will asked, on edge.

"They're here."

"Where?"

"One of them was just spotted two blocks over."

Will cursed and ran his hand through his hair. "Which one?"

"I don't know, sir—"

"Find out which one!"

"Yes, sir."

My heartbeat echoed in my ears.

I wanted to know who was spotted just as much as Will did.

We waited. The agent stepped on the gas.

"Copy," he said again. To Will he said, "It was unit three."

We neared another intersection. The light was green. The agent swerved around a car, and the tires squealed. I clutched the door handle to keep me steady and because the closer I was to it, the easier it would be to pull it open so I could escape when the time was right.

"Give me an update," Will said. "I want a location on Trev and a sweep of the town, a clearing of the freeway—"

I glanced out the window, searching for a familiar face. My boys were here. We just had to find one another.

The car raced through the intersection. I pressed my face against the glass, looking ahead for a place to bail.

Something on the rooftop of a building on the next street corner caught my eye. A figure, arms propped on the edge, a rifle trained on us. At first I thought it was one of Will's men, covering our getaway, but then there was a *pop* from below our car, and the driver swerved.

Another *pop*. The sharp, cutting sound of metal against concrete. The tires had been blown out.

There was no way this car was going to make it out of town now.

I glanced over at Will. Jaw clenched, hands tight, he looked on the verge of hitting something. But below that was a sadness, a fear, etched into the tiny lines around his eyes—he knew he was losing.

As we crossed the next intersection, and I looked past Will out the window, I saw Sam. I saw him behind the wheel of a black cargo van. Saw him just seconds before he drove that van straight into our car.

32

THERE WAS A MOMENT WHERE NOT
even the seat belt could keep me grounded. It was as if I were floating.
My hair swung forward, blinding me, so that I couldn't tell which
way was up and which way was down.

Shards of glass bit into my skin.

When the car landed, the impact slammed me into the frame of
the door. Blood ran from a new wound at my temple. It took me a second to realize the car was on its side, that my door was on the ground.

The car slid that way for several more feet, filling my ears with the
hideous scraping sound of crunched metal and scratched pavement.

When the car came to a rest, it teetered before flipping over on its
roof, suspending us from our seats.

"Anna?" Will croaked. He cut his belt loose with a pocketknife and scrambled over the twisted metal of the roof to my side. "Are you okay?"

"If you're smart," I said, "you'll start running now and get a head start."

He frowned and met my eyes.

It was a test. I think he knew it.

I wanted to see what he would do. If he ran, then his life and his business and *his* Branch were clearly more important than family—than me.

I wouldn't have blamed him.

He threaded his fingers through my hair and pushed it back behind my ear. He kissed my forehead, and I shrank away. "Everything I've ever done has been with your best interests at heart," he said.

A car door opened and slammed shut somewhere in the street. Tires screeched to a halt. People were shouting. Someone said there was a gun.

"You did all the wrong things," I said.

He pursed his mouth, somber. "I know."

He kicked my door open, crawled out, and ran.

———

As the shouting and fighting grew outside of the car, I clutched my seat belt, the nylon material digging into my chest. I pressed my eyes closed.

I could let Will go.

Or I could kill him.

These were my options, neither of them good. I didn't want to kill him, but there'd already been too much death, caused by Will and the Branch. And letting him go would result in so much more.

This would never be over as long as the Branch was operational.

We would never be free.

What I wanted more than anything was some semblance of a normal life, of safety. I wanted to wake in the morning, nothing more than a girl with a boy beside her. A boy she loved.

I deserved those things.

Sam deserved those things.

And Cas. And Nick. And even Trev.

So had Dani.

I freed myself from my seat belt, and still shaky with adrenaline, scrambled to the front seat, to the dead agent crushed against the steering wheel, and stole his gun.

I kicked the passenger-side door till it gave way, and slipped into the light. Fresh air filled my lungs.

I turned.

The intersection was a pile of wreckage and a buzzing, flailing mass of agents getting their asses kicked by the boys.

My boys.

I locked eyes with Sam across the undercarriage of the car. His face was covered in bruises and scrapes and deliberate cuts, as if someone had tortured him one slice at a time.

His lip was split on the side. His dark hair was covered in old and new blood.

An agent made a run for him, but Sam was quicker and slammed a fist into the man's face. The agent fell over backward.

Wait for me, he said with a look. *Give me two minutes, and I'll come with you.*

I can't.

I didn't have any minutes to spare.

I ran in the direction Will had disappeared.

If I were him, where would I go?

The airport.

To his waiting jet.

It was safe to assume, I thought, that Will would have to find some other kind of transportation to reach the airport. If he still had his cell phone, he'd call in another agent. If he didn't, he'd probably steal a vehicle or—

I heard the distant sound of metal rattling, as if a garage door were opening.

Following the sound, I took the next street, running as fast as the grips on my shoes would allow me. The streets had been plowed, but there were patches of ice here and there, and rivets of slush to navigate.

I slowed when I neared a car garage, the large bay door open, revealing the inside. Chipped and faded lettering at the top of the building said it was once Nate & Frank's Garage. Now, instead of broken cars inside its interior, there were rows of four-wheelers, dirt bikes, motorcycles, and two black Suburbans.

A showroom? Or, more likely, a Branch stock garage.

The other bay doors were closed, hiding whatever else was inside. I couldn't see Will from my vantage point, so I brought my gun up.

A woman stopped me. "Can I help you?" she asked in a tone that said she didn't plan on helping me with anything.

I sized her up. She was lanky, with sharp eyes and a straight nose and an even sharper mouth.

Judging by her clothes—black cargo pants, black undershirt, black armored vest—she wasn't simply a woman manning Nate & Frank's Garage. She was a Branch agent.

I peered over her shoulder in time to see Will shoot past us on a four-wheeler.

I watched which direction he went, giving the lanky woman the chance to catch me off guard. She threw a left-handed punch to my cheek that spun me around and landed me on the pavement.

I lost my gun.

On all fours, as I tried to catch my breath, she kicked me in the ribs. I cringed and rolled to my side. She wound a hand into the collar of my shirt and raised me off the floor just enough to punch me again in the face. The coppery taste of blood coated the back of my teeth.

She pulled a blade from a sheath tucked in her boot and brought it down like a hammer. I caught her wrist at the last second, but my arms shook as the blade pressed closer.

Look for a weakness.

With all her energy focused on the knife, she left her side wide open. Using my grip on her wrist as leverage, I brought my knee up and into her ribs. She cried out and shrank away.

I scooped up my gun, shot. One bullet to the head. She dropped where she stood.

I slid my gun in the waistband of my pants and ran to the row of four-wheelers. There were keys already in the ignition.

"Thank you," I muttered to no one. I climbed on and started it up, throttling the gas.

I sped out the bay door.

Wind cut through my clothes and bit at my exposed skin. The tire tracks of the four-wheeler were easier to follow than Will's footprints, and before long, I'd left the town behind. I followed the tracks through a patch of dense woods and came out the other side on a railroad line. I could just make out Will's figure up ahead, maybe a mile and a half away at most.

I twisted the throttle and the four-wheeler shot forward. Will noticed me with a quick glance over his shoulder.

The tracks curved inward, hugging a sandhill covered in patches of snow. Rays of sunlight shone over the top, blinding me, so that when I finally drove into the shadow of the hill, I didn't notice the figure leaping toward me until it was too late.

Will knocked me from my seat. We slammed onto the ground, and the four-wheeler careened down the tracks before hitting one of the rails and flipping over on itself.

I bucked Will off me and reached for my gun, but he caught me with a backhanded slap, and the gun flew out of my grasp. Stars winked in my vision. I scurried over the tracks, fingers scraping against the old railroad ties. A loose one wobbled beneath me, and I felt the sharp pressure of a sliver in my index finger and another in my thumb. I bit back the pain and reached for the gun, just inches away, when a shot went off behind me and a burning, flaring sensation raced up my thigh, vibrating through every nerve in my body.

I screamed and clutched at my leg, my hand coming away wet with blood.

Will loomed over me. He had a cell phone in his hand. "Riley," he said, "I'm on the railroad tracks about a mile south of Neason Road. I need a truck."

Tears streamed down my face. My leg throbbed with the pulse of my heart, and the pain only seemed to get worse, sinking through muscle and bone, aching in a place that was both physical and mental.

"Have they been taken care of?" Will asked. He waited for the reply. "Well, get on it, then."

He hung up and slid the phone in his pocket. He crouched beside me. "Let me see," he said and pushed my hands away. "I tried to get a clean shot, something that wouldn't cause too much permanent damage." He pressed against the wound with his fingers, and I arched back, sobbing as the pain laced its way to the center of my gut.

"You'll be fine," he decided. "Look at me, Anna."

I sucked in a breath and glanced over at him. "I will take care of you. I promise," he said, the sharp angles of his face softening in the golden light. "I fixed you once before. I can do it again."

"Don't kill them," I said. "The boys. Please."

Will shook his head. "You're better off without them. We all are. I never should have let Connor talk me into rehabilitating them. We should have cut our losses and—"

I wrapped my hand around the loose railroad tie, sand gritting beneath my fingernails.

Anger and pain and heartache and hope all mixed together and cannoned up my body.

I swung, hitting Will on the side of the head. He fell back. I grabbed my gun, buried the burn of the gunshot in my leg, and stood to my feet.

Will looked up at me, sadness etched in the space between his eyes. He parted his lips as if he wanted to say something, but didn't even know where to start.

Instead, he said only, "I'm sorry, Anna," right before I pulled the trigger.

Sam found me first. I don't know how long I sat there staring at Uncle Will, but it seemed like a long time. Like forever.

The snow turned black with Will's blood. The wind slowed and the clouds opened up and snow began to fall. I couldn't feel my fingers or my toes. I couldn't feel my injured leg, which seemed a good thing at the time but was sure to be a problem later.

When Sam appeared around the bend in the railroad track, I thought for a moment he was a figment of my imagination, that I was dying. Or dead already.

He started running when he spotted me, pausing only long enough to make sure Will was no longer a threat before grabbing me in his arms and squeezing until I couldn't breathe.

"Are you okay? Did he—"

I took Sam's face in my hands and kissed him. If I lost feeling in every other part of my body, I'd be all right as long as I could feel this: his lips on mine, his breath on my face, his fingers brushing the tears from my chin.

"I love you," I said when I pulled away.

He pressed his forehead against mine and ran his hands through my snarled hair, his fingertips kneading at the base of my neck. "I love you, too."

I smiled and closed my eyes, all the tension running from my body.

And then I was out.

My head lolled against Sam's chest. I thought I could feel his arm beneath my legs, and the other wrapped around my waist. I heard the beating of his heart. Or maybe that was mine.

I couldn't be sure.

"She all right?" That was Nick.

"I think so. We have to get her to a hospital. Will shot her."

"Ginger prick," Nick said.

Sam tightened his hold on me. "Did you take care of—"

"Yeah," Nick cut in. "Cas and Trev moved Arthur to a safe place."

"And Riley?"

He hadn't ever shown with the truck Will had asked for, and I'd waited. I'd been ready.

"No sign of him. I hope he ran," Nick finally said. "Good fucking riddance."

33

I WAS IN AND OUT FOR SEVERAL
days. The few times I was *in*, I heard the distant murmuring of nurses,
sometimes a doctor. *Shock*, they said. *Infection. Poor girl*, they said.

I wondered if it was a way of my body telling me it needed rest.
Not just because it'd been shot. But because it'd been through too
much too soon.

When I finally opened my eyes and felt well enough to speak,
Sam was by my side.

"Hey," he said as sunlight poured from the window over his
shoulder.

"Curtains," I mumbled, my throat raw.

He got up and tugged the curtains closed, plunging the room
into semidarkness. "Better?"

I opened my eyes slowly. "Much."

Seeing Sam beside my bed was enough to put a smile on my face.

"What happened?" I asked. "Did the gunshot wound heal all right?"

"Drink this first." He offered me a bottle of water. I started to object, but he shook his head, so I drank. And then guzzled the whole thing down. I guess I was thirstier than I thought.

After, with Sam's help, I managed to pull myself into an upright position. When he settled back into the chair at my bedside, I looked him over. The skin beneath his eyes was shadowed and heavy. Stubble covered his face, hiding some of the cuts and bruises that were still healing. His hair stuck up at the crown, like he hadn't showered yet today. Maybe not the day before, either. There was a long scrape running from the side of his neck, disappearing beneath the collar of his navy shirt.

"How are you?" I asked.

He let out a breath. "How am *I*? I'm not the one who got shot."

I looked down at my legs and wiggled my toes beneath the blanket. Everything seemed to be in working order. Thank God. "How long was I out?"

"Five days."

"Five days?" I shrieked.

"You had a minor infection. The doctors took care of it. You're fine now."

I laid my head back against the mountain of pillows beneath me.

"And Nick and Cas?"

"They're fine. They're getting something to eat right now."

"My dad?"

Sam went quiet. That old, guarded expression I knew so well returned.

"Sam."

He shifted his gaze to the floor, folded his hands together. "They wiped his memory before we got to him."

Crying first thing upon waking after a five-day coma didn't seem like the proper way to start the recuperation process. And my sides still hurt more than I could describe, and crying would only make it worse. So I bit my lip until the sensation died away.

Dad, I thought. *I'm so sorry.*

"Where is he?" I finally asked.

"He's safe."

"Where is he, Sam?"

"A place for senior citizens. He seems happy there."

"You put him in a home?"

Sam straightened, gave me a sad, regretful look. He took in a long breath before answering. "He has lung cancer, Anna."

"What? But—"

"He let it slip when I called him, when we were looking into the coded program."

When I'd seen him after leaving the boys, I'd thought he looked unwell. I hadn't realized it was that bad.

"He'll be taken care of," Sam went on. "He had money set aside for retirement, so the bills are covered. He's in a good place."

I nodded. After everything he'd been through, a home for senior citizens did seem like a vacation.

"I have to see him."

"You will. Soon. You have to rest for now. Geez, Anna, take a break. Everything has been taken care of."

We fell into silence. The machines behind me beeped and chugged.

"Thanks," I said after a while. "For taking care of my dad."

Sam shrugged. "He took care of us while we were in the farmhouse lab."

Mention of the lab brought on another thought. A question I wanted to ask but was afraid to admit to Sam that I cared what the answer was.

He met my eyes, and a veil of worry eased over his face. "Trev?" he asked quietly.

"What happened with him?"

A baby cried out in the hallway, making Sam and me pause. When it was quiet again, he said, "He helped us escape and then plot your rescue. He helped save you, but I haven't seen him since that day. I'm assuming he's all right."

"Trev was the one on the roof with the rifle, wasn't he? The one who shot out the tires?"

"Yeah."

"Were you guys at least nice to him?"

Sam smiled. "What do you think?"

"I think Nick was an asshole, Cas gave him a hard time, and you gave him the silent treatment."

Sam didn't say anything.

"You did, didn't you?"

The door to my room opened. I thought it'd be a nurse to check on me, but it was Cas and Nick. I was glad to see them. I wasn't ready to answer questions for the hospital staff. Or to be poked and prodded.

"How long has she been awake?" Nick asked, the ever-present scowl deepening on his face. "How come you didn't call us?"

"She just woke up," Sam said.

"Just now," I said.

Cas came straight over to my bedside. "My love. I'm so glad you're awake." And then he planted his lips on mine, cradling my head in his hands.

I pushed him off. "Cas!"

Sam reached across me and whacked Cas on the side of the head. "Quit being an idiot."

Cas frowned. "Don't you remember? She said she didn't love you. She realized she loved me instead."

I rolled my eyes. "Nice try."

He grinned and pulled himself into the windowsill across the room, an open bag of chips in his hand. "You can't blame a guy."

I couldn't stop the smile that spread across my face, even while I said, "You are so irritating sometimes."

"Irritatingly adorable."

When I looked again at Sam, I caught some silent conversation going on between him and Nick. Finally Sam broke the stare-down and glanced over at me. "Cas and I are going for a walk. You'll be okay?"

I nodded, eyeing Nick. "Sure."

"Since when do we take walks together?" Cas asked.

Sam ignored the question and pushed him toward the door. When they were gone, Nick came over and dropped into Sam's abandoned chair.

"Hey," I said.

Nick folded his hands together and cracked his knuckles. "I remember," he said, his voice quiet and raw. "I remember everything."

I sat up straighter. "Everything? How long? I mean . . ."

Another *pop* of his knuckles. "Long enough." He sighed, ran his hand through his hair. Not that it did any good. It settled back in place, waves of dark hair curling around his ears. "I remember the first time I saw you with a bruise on your face. You were just a kid. And you'd been crying, and you wouldn't look at me. You wouldn't look at any of us." He shook his head. "Your dad was already breaking you."

"Nick—" I started, but he cut in before I could finish.

"It was my idea to wipe your memory. Back before the farmhouse. I told Dani she should let your uncle do it, make you forget the shit your dad put you through, because *I* wanted to forget, every single day of my life, what my dad had done to me."

I didn't say anything, because I didn't know what to say. My memory being wiped so often, at such an early age, was part of the reason I'd been so confused the night I'd killed my parents.

But none of this would have happened if it wasn't for Will and the Branch he'd created.

I blamed him more than anything.

"I remember making you a promise that day," Nick continued. "I told you I would look out for you, and clearly I failed."

"You don't have to—"

He held up a hand. "Calm down. I'm not going to start spilling my soul. I just wanted to say that I am sorry for being such a dick at the farmhouse."

I whipped the blanket back and lunged at him, wrapping my arms around his neck. Immediately, he stiffened, his arms stuck at his side, unmoving. But then he relaxed, and his arms came up, winding loosely around me.

"Now lie back down," he ordered. "Jesus Christ. You just got shot."

I smiled as he helped me into bed. I laid my head back against the pillows and closed my eyes.

I pictured the box of paper cranes still beneath the bed at our last house, the cabin we'd had to leave after we'd seen Riley on the grocery store security footage. I'd forgotten to grab them. Now that the Branch was broken, I wondered if it was safe to return there. If we could, I'd hang the paper cranes from the ceiling in my next room and watch them dance in the night.

34

USING CRUTCHES, I HOBBLED DOWN
the hallway of Cherry Creek Manor to room 214. I peered inside the
open doorway at a man sitting in an easy chair staring out the
window.

"Dad?" I said.

The man turned his head toward me. He stared at my face.
Looked at my crutches. "Anna?" he said.

A renewed sense of hope and excitement came over me. "You
remember me?" I asked.

He gave me a sheepish smile. "The nurse told me you were coming today."

"Oh. Right." I crutched my way into the room and sat in the
chair across from him. His room was a generous size, with a private

bathroom and deck that overlooked the massive gardens. The gardens were covered in snow now, of course, but I could see hints of what it would look like in the spring. Pretty enough to spend an entire day sketching it.

"How are you?" I asked once I'd set the crutches aside.

Dad shrugged and then coughed, and then coughed some more. I pushed myself up and hopped to his side, patting his back. "Do you need some water?"

Still coughing, he waved me away. "No. I'm fine. Just a spell, is all."

I sat back down. "When do you start treatments? For the cancer?"

He lifted a shoulder. "I'm old. Why would I want to go through that? It isn't as if I won't die soon anyway. Dying is inevitable."

"But it might give you a few more years."

"Years full of treatments and nausea? And achy bones? No, thank you." He looked at me for a long time, head tilted slightly. "How are you? Sam told me you were in the hospital recuperating from a gunshot wound. Who would shoot a young woman?"

My own uncle, I thought.

"I'm fine. Much better already."

He nodded, but the look on his face said my answer wasn't explanatory enough. I just didn't have the energy to go into further detail, so I changed the subject.

"Are you happy here?"

He thought for a long time before finally saying, "Yes. I think so. I like the people here. I feel happy."

Maybe Sam was right.

Maybe this was the best place for him.

We talked for a while longer about nothing in particular—the weather, the food Dad was eating, the news. It was odd for me just sitting with him, chatting. My dad and I had never been big on small talk. But I enjoyed it now.

"Well, I should go." I slowly rose to my feet. "I'll check in soon, okay? And if you need me, you have my number."

I crutched my way to the door.

"Anna?" Dad called. I paused in the doorway. "I love you."

My eyes burned with the sudden need to cry. I sucked it up.

"I love you, too."

He smiled before turning away and resumed looking out the window.

35

DESPITE THE WEEKS THAT HAD PASSED since I'd killed Will, since the Branch had broken itself into nothing but scattered pieces, I was still finding it difficult to order a cup of coffee without overanalyzing the people in the shop. Without placing the exits and alternate exits in my head.

Of all the habits one could form, those weren't so bad.

The barista behind the counter handed me my coffee, and I turned to the bar to add a few packets of sugar and cream when I nearly ran into someone who'd been standing directly behind me.

"Excuse me," I said. "I'm sorry."

"It's all right."

I looked up at the sound of the familiar voice.

"Trev."

"Do you have a minute?"

I glanced out the front windows at the sedan sitting across the street. Sam, Nick, and Cas were waiting inside. I could see Cas dancing to the music that must have been blasting from the stereo system. And Nick scowling at him.

Sam stared at the coffee shop.

"How did you get past Sam?" I asked Trev.

A prideful smile teased at the corners of his mouth. "I'm not as useless as you seem to think I am."

I checked the car again.

"It'll just take a second," Trev said.

"All right."

He led me to a table along the far wall. We both danced around each other, trying to claim the seat that faced the door. I won.

"What do you want?" I said, clutching the paper coffee cup in my hands. It was nearly scalding, but if I needed a weapon quickly, burning coffee was my best bet without drawing too much attention.

I didn't know what this was or who Trev might have with him, so I wanted to be prepared, even if my heart said to calm the hell down. He'd helped save me, after all. More than once. Things had been so good these last few weeks that I couldn't help but expect something bad to happen.

"I just wanted to see you," he answered, adjusting the cuffs of his wool trench coat. The collar stuck up high around his neck, like a shield. His hair was shorter than when I last saw him, trimmed neatly, swept to one side.

"See me for what?"

"To say good-bye."

I frowned. "Are you going somewhere?"

He tapped lightly at the table, as if to stall while he rehearsed what he wanted to get out.

"After you guys first escaped headquarters back in October, I started digging into my past. Do you remember me telling you about the girl I thought I was working to keep safe? That she was the reason I was with the Branch?"

I nodded.

"Well, I went looking for her. And I found her. She was real after all."

I straightened. "And?"

"She barely remembered me. And while I spent all those years being treated with anti-aging serums, she aged normally. She got married. She had a kid."

He looked away, toward a couple at the table across from us. They seemed oblivious to everything around them.

When he turned back to me, I saw the old Trev, and I saw that look on his face, the lightbulb moment that meant he'd found a quote in his vast collection that would fit perfectly for the moment.

But as quickly as it'd come, the expression faded, and I realized that I was no longer the person he liked to share his quotes with. Whatever this one had been, I would never know it.

"I ruined what I had with you guys for a girl who had moved on. And now..." He trailed off and pulled his hands back, tucking them in his lap.

I suddenly went on alert.

"There's that, too," he said, gesturing at me. "It doesn't matter how many times I try to prove my loyalty to you. You'll never trust me again."

He was right, but I said, "I'm sorry," anyway.

He shook his head and pulled a cell phone from his pocket. "I have a gift for you." He tapped something into the screen before turning the phone around so I could see the image. It was a button that said simply DETONATE.

"What's this?"

"An end," he said.

"To what?"

"The Branch."

I frowned. "I don't understand."

He leaned forward and lowered his voice. "Push the button and you'll see." He swept out of the chair, came around the table, and hugged me. It was a tentative hug for a timid friend. I let go of my coffee to return it.

"I miss you, Anna. Every single day."

When he pulled away, a part of me, the part that had been best friends with him for so many years, seemed to pull away, too.

I didn't want him to go, but at the same time, I knew he couldn't stay. He couldn't ever be part of our group again.

"Take care of yourself," he said.

He walked out the front door, as if to prove to Sam he still had the ability to move around without him noticing. As if to say, *See, I could have done something terrible, but I didn't.*

When Sam saw Trev, he got out of the car and raced across the street.

I hurried out the front door. "It's fine," I said.

Trev kept going, hands tucked in his pockets. He didn't look back.

Later that night, I set the cell phone Trev had given me in the center of the table. We gathered around and stared at it. The red button was just an image on the screen, but it was so much more than that.

We knew the risks were huge. We knew it could be a trap.

"Ready?" I said.

The boys nodded.

I pressed the button.

36

SAM TUGGED ME CLOSER, HIS ARM TUCKED beneath my head. I snuggled into the crook of his neck, breathing in deeply. He still smelled like autumn, even though it was mid-May and everything was drenched in fresh air and new life.

I ran my hand up his bare stomach, tracing the lines between his abs with my index finger. He shuddered, which only fueled my need to keep going. I crawled on top of him, pinning him down.

A lazy smile crept on his face.

"I fully plan on taking advantage of you, and you don't get any say in the matter."

"Oh, no?" In one quick movement, he wrapped his arms around me and rolled me over, pinning me on my back.

I laughed. He kissed me. Once. Twice.

I reached down for the tie on his board shorts and tugged on one of the laces. This was how we spent most afternoons now, and it was absolutely, positively, the best way to waste a day.

The Branch was gone. With one little app, one little red button, we'd detonated the bombs Trev had planted, and the Branch headquarters had gone up in smoke. So had the warehouse in Port Cadia and the lab in Indiana. The media had covered the explosions for weeks afterward as they theorized how the locations were connected. It became even more of a lucrative story when any and all officials involved in the case refused to talk.

Although we were almost certain the Branch was completely wiped out, we had yet to confirm what had happened to Riley. Who knew where that weasel was hiding. Hopefully in some hole far, far away, never to bother us again.

Sam's fingers edged beneath the hem of my tank top. My stomach filled with butterflies as his fingertips glided across my skin. He kissed me once and pulled back. "I have something for you."

I frowned. "What?"

He rolled away from me and reached beneath the bed. He came back a second later with a book. Black hardcover. No writing on the front. I sucked in a breath.

"Is it—"

"It's not the same one," he said quickly. "But I got one as close to it as I could."

I took the journal from him and opened it. The pages were thick hand-pressed paper, just like the one he had gotten me for my seventeenth birthday. And as before, he'd written something on the first page.

To Anna and a new beginning.

—Sam

Tears burned in the depths of my eyes. I lunged at him, wrapping my arms around him. He hugged me back.

"Thank you," I said. "It's perfect."

"You're welcome." He moved as if to kiss me but was cut off by Nick's shouting from downstairs.

"Sam! Get your ass down here! Cas seems to think he can fly."

Sam sank next to me and closed his eyes. "I'm sorry," he muttered.

"Don't be."

He kissed my forehead, traced a thumb across my lips. "I'll be back."

I smiled. "I'll be here."

He left the room, thudded down the stairs. I could hear him and Nick trying to convince Cas to get off the roof of the porch.

I lay on my back, closed my eyes. A warm summer breeze blew in through the open window. I arched my bare feet, the sun warming my legs.

"Cas!" Sam yelled.

There was a *thud* a second later, then an *umph*. "Ohhh crap," Cas groaned.

"You're such a goddamn idiot," Nick said.

"At least I'm good-looking," Cas countered.

Nick tsked. "Except no one likes a dumbass."

Cas laughed. "That would explain why you get zero action."

A scuffling noise followed. Cas laughed again, the sound fading into the background.

I hadn't shot a gun in weeks. I hadn't needed to run from agents. I hadn't had to steal a car or fight anyone with my bare hands. This break was the best thing for all of us, and I didn't ever want it to end.

Nothing was permanent. I knew that. The boys still had a lot of things they wanted to find out about their old lives. Cas had remembered a few details about his grandma—that she'd raised him—and we'd been taking the steps to find her. Nick wanted revenge on his father, though whether or not he was serious was unknown to all of us. I hoped he wasn't.

Whatever our futures held, I was sure of one thing: We were family. The boys and me. And nothing we found out about our pasts would change that.

I clutched the new journal to my chest and looked up at the ceiling, as the paper cranes danced in the breeze.

ACKNOWLEDGMENTS

It takes an army to create a book, and my list of people to thank reflects that.

First and foremost, my editor, Julie Scheina, who I am convinced would win the Editor Olympics if there were such a thing. She is clever and wise and kind and all the other adjectives that would be listed under *awesome* in a thesaurus. My books are a million times better because of her savvy ability to ask all the right questions.

To my agent, Joanna Volpe, who is a badass businesswoman, but also a kind and caring advocate. Without her, I fear I would be a colossal mess most days. I can't imagine building a career in this industry without her at my side. I thank my lucky stars for her every day.

Special thanks must go out to Pam Garfinkel and Danielle Barthel, for answering my eighty billion questions/e-mails, for keeping everything running smoothly, and for being all-around awesome.

To Pouya and Kathleen, for their love and support of *Altered* and *Erased*!

To everyone else at Little, Brown and New Leaf Lit, some whom I have yet to meet, but who are no less important!

To Patricia Riley and Danielle Ellison, for all the Skype chats, and tweets and texts and e-mails, that helped me through the rough patches. You guys know how and when to cheer me up and I am forever indebted to you for it.

To Adam Silvera, for all the love. Although we met only last year, it seems like we've been friends forever. I'm so glad I ended up sitting across from you at that restaurant in NYC. If I hadn't, I would not have you in my life, and I can't picture it without you.

To all the readers and bloggers, for their support of *Altered* and *Erased*, and Anna and the boys! I write for the readers, and I love hearing from you all, because it makes working in the editing trenches so much easier.

To my family and friends, for their endless encouragement! You guys are amazing. To the grandparents, especially, for the hours and hours of babysitting!

To my husband, JV, my bestest friend in the whole entire world, I could not have written these books without you. You know how to cheer me up, you know how to make me laugh, and you know exactly how to make me feel special when I'm feeling anything but.

And last, and no less important, my chair, for being one comfy son of a bitch. My butt thanks you.